OUR DAY WILL COME

When handsome American airman Ben Greenwood walks into the Quiet Woman pub, the landlord's pretty daughter Betty Yeardley is immediately attracted to him. But Betty is promised to Eddie Simpson, who has been missing in action for two years. With a stocking thief putting the villagers of Midchester on edge, and Eddie's parents putting pressure on Betty to keep her promise, she is forced to fight her growing feelings for Ben.

Books by Sally Quilford
in the Linford Romance Library:

THE SECRET OF HELENA'S BAY
BELLA'S VINEYARD
A COLLECTOR OF HEARTS
MY TRUE COMPANION
AN IMITATION OF LOVE
SUNLIT SECRETS
MISTLETOE MYSTERY

SALLY QUILFORD

OUR DAY
WILL COME

Complete and Unabridged

LINFORD
Leicester

First published in Great Britain in 2012

First Linford Edition
published 2013

A catalogue record for this book is available
from the British Library.

ISBN 978–1–4448–1578–8

Published by
F. A. Thorpe (Publishing)
Anstey, Leicestershire

Set by Words & Graphics Ltd.
Anstey, Leicestershire
Printed and bound in Great Britain by
T. J. International Ltd., Padstow, Cornwall

This book is printed on acid-free paper

1944

It was about noon when Peg Bradbourne walked into the pub. She sat down on her usual stool in the Quiet Woman. It was in the ladies' lounge, but at the bar. Peg liked to keep an eye on what was happening in the saloon where all the men usually sat, nursing half pints of ale. The pub was not very busy yet, but would soon fill up when the lunchtime crowd arrived.

'It's happened again!' Peg was an elderly lady, but had a real sparkle in her eyes, showing a keen mind. It was rumoured that she had been something of a sleuth in her day.

'What's happened now, Peg?' In a well-rehearsed move, the landlord's daughter, Betty Yeardley, put an open bottle of stout and a glass in front of Peg.

'My stockings have been stolen from

the washing line.'

'Not again! How many times is that?'

'Three for me. Myrtle Simpson says it's happened to her twice. A few other women in the village have had it happen at least once. Honestly, I'd darned those stockings a dozen times, but there was some wear left in them.'

As it was wartime, people had to learn to be very creative about mending their clothes.

'Did you tell the constable, Peg?'

'Constable Fisher is about as much use as a chocolate fireguard.' Peg rolled her eyes. 'It's not his fault,' she added, more sympathetically. 'All the young men are off fighting, and those left aren't exactly the best of the best. Bless them, they do all they can, but old Cyril has lumbago and young Graham is deaf in one ear. Which is just as well for them, or they'd be sent off to fight, too.'

'When do you think it's happening?' Betty asked. 'The stockings being stolen, I mean.'

'I'm not sure. I put the washing out

very early, and went in to get on with my chores. I read my post and then had a cup of tea. An hour might have passed before I went back outside to check the washing.'

'So it's in broad daylight?'

'Well, yes. Only Mrs Baker leaves her washing out all night.' Peg sniffed disapprovingly. 'But she does have a lot of children, so I suppose she does it when she can.'

That, thought Betty with a smile, was Peg's way. She might start off criticising someone, but she could never follow it through. She always ended by empathising in some way. Peg had a forgiving nature, even for the least likeable villagers.

'I still think you should tell the constable.'

'Tell the constable what?' a voice called from the bar room.

It was an American accent. Betty turned and looked up into a pair of ice-blue eyes.

'I, er, we're having a problem with

ladies' stockings being stolen from washing lines.'

Betty blushed. It seemed an intimate subject to be sharing with a stranger, and a very handsome one at that. He was dressed in the uniform of an American airman.

'Can I help you, sir?'

'Thank you. I'd like a half pint of your best ale, please.'

Betty smiled. It sounded very quaint the way he said it.

'Did I get it wrong?' he asked, as if sensing her amusement.

'Oh, no, you were exactly right.' Betty picked up a clean glass and started to fill it from the pump.

'Phew! I've been practising with the guys up at the hospital.'

'Ah, you're from Bedlington Hall.'

Bedlington Hall had been utilised as a military hospital since the beginning of the war. It was mostly for recuperating soldiers and airmen. There was an airbase some way out of Midchester, which also had lots of American airmen. They seldom ventured to Midchester, preferring the bigger towns of Shrewsbury and Hereford.

'That's right, ma'am. I managed to get myself shot down over France. Now I'm trying out the old legs again.'

'How is that working out?'

'I don't know, but I reckon that smile is the best painkiller I've ever seen.'

Betty blushed and busied herself polishing glasses.

'So you've got yourself a sinister stocking stealer?'

Betty and Peg burst out laughing.

'It seems so, which is really annoying,' Peg replied. 'Even if I can see the funny side, we can't afford to lose pairs of stockings.'

'Well, if you ever need any . . . ' The young airman stopped, noticing how Betty froze. He was no doubt as aware as she how stockings and chocolate were often used as gifts in romances between American servicemen and British girls.

'I'm sorry, ma'am, I didn't mean it

5

that way. What I meant was that I know a guy who can get some.'

'What a pity,' Peg commented from across the bar. 'I was hoping to be compromised by such a handsome young man. You'd better tell me your name before Betty hits you with the tea towel.'

'I'm Benedict Greenwood, ma'am, but my friends call me Ben.'

'It's nice to make your acquaintance, Ben. I'm Peg Bradbourne and this pretty young girl is Betty Yeardley. Her father owns this pub, so you'd better be nice to her.'

'I can't imagine anyone ever not being nice to her.'

'It's a very nice offer — about the stockings,' she said shyly, 'but I'm sure we can manage.'

'What's that about stockings?'

Betty had been so engrossed in Ben that she hadn't noticed Herbie Potter, the postman, entering the pub along with his friend, Len Simpson. Herbie put the post for the pub on to the bar.

'Morning, Mr Potter. Mr Simpson. The usual?'

Herbie nodded curtly.

'Peg's stockings have been stolen this morning.' Betty popping the letters under the counter. 'I've told her she should speak to the constable.'

'I'm sure the constable has more things to worry about than ladies' stockings,' Herbie said dismissively.

'They're not cheap to buy, nor easy to get hold of, Herbie,' Peg said in preaching tones. 'Stealing stockings may sound amusing to you men, but it's a very unpleasant act in these days of rationing.'

'Betty,' Len Simpson said once his drink was in front of him, 'are there any letters amongst those from Eddie?'

His voice told her that he disapproved of her not checking the post first.

Betty picked the letters back up and sifted through them.

'No, nothing,' she said, shamefaced.

If truth be known, she had stopped

looking quite a while before, but only when it seemed fruitless to do so.

'I'm sure that if there were news, you'd hear first.'

'I doubt it. He'd want to tell his best girl that he's alive, I should think.' Len looked from Betty to the American then back again with meaning.

Betty blushed even more. It was too bad that she could not even speak to another young man without Len thinking she was being unfaithful to Eddie.

'Is this Eddie your sweetheart?' Ben asked when she went to get his empty glass. Herbie and Len had gone to a corner table to chat.

'Yes.' She lowered her voice. 'But he's been missing in action for two years. Of course I hope he's alive, but the longer it goes on . . . '

'It must be very hard.'

'It is, of course, but worse for his parents.'

'Maybe you could tell me about it some time.'

'I'm sure you'd find it very boring. Do you have a sweetheart at home?'

Please say yes, Betty thought. It would make things much easier for her.

'I did, but I got a letter from her about six months ago, breaking it off. She'd met someone else, and married him.'

'Oh, that's awful. I'm sorry.'

'Don't be.'

'When did you have your accident, Ben?' Betty felt they ought to get on safer ground.

'About six months ago. I was on a hospital ship for a while, and then they brought me to this beautiful village. It's my first day out for two months.'

It didn't take much for Betty to work out that the crash had come soon after Ben's sweetheart broke his heart. It made her think of Eddie. He could be out there somewhere, cold, injured, banking on her waiting for him to return.

The pub began to fill up, so Betty had no more time to talk to Ben. Her father, Tom, joined her behind the bar. The talk was, naturally, about the Stocking Stealer. There were suggestions that the Home Guard start to look out for prowlers on their travels during the night.

'With most of the stockings being stolen in the mornings,' Herbie Potter reasoned, 'it must mean that someone is hanging around at night.'

'If there was a stranger lurking, we'd see them,' Tom Yeardley said. 'We all know each other here, and with all respect to our brave American here, we notice strangers.'

'That could mean it's one of us!' Peg called from her place at the bar.

'No-one in Midchester would do a thing like that,' Len Simpson said. 'We've had our share of eccentrics here, and a bit of petty thievery in the past, but stealing stockings, well, it's not the Midchester way.'

'We've had murders in Midchester,' Peg reminded him. 'You can't get more destructive than that!'

'All done by outsiders, Peg. Not locals.'

'Not all of them,' Peg muttered into her glass. She pushed it across the bar and gestured to Betty to fetch another bottle of stout.

'You've had murders here?' Ben, who had remained quiet during the conversation, was all agog.

'Oh, yes, dear.'

'Then I guess you should be grateful that, so far, only stockings are being stolen,' Ben said. 'Such things usually escalate. My dad is a policeman in New York, and he deals with a lot of these crimes. I hate to say it, but what's happened so far does seem to be aimed at the nice ladies in this village.'

The bar went quiet at that.

'I'm sure no-one wants to hurt our women,' Len Simpson said.

But it had given them all something to think about.

'It'll be outsiders,' Herbie Potter said after a few minutes. He looked Tom Yeardley in the eye. 'Servicemen bring a lot of problems with them. Some pubs and municipal parks have banned them.'

His meaning was clear.

'They are also fighting bravely to try and beat Hitler,' Tom protested. 'And I can assure Mr . . . '

'Captain Ben Greenwood, at your service, sir.' Ben replied.

'I can assure Captain Greenwood that, as long as I'm landlord of this pub, he and his brave compatriots are very welcome here.'

Tom rested two hands on the bar, staring out over the assembled drinkers.

'Listen to us all, safe and comfortable in Midchester, gossiping over our ale and pointing fingers at people! We should never forget what those lads are doing for us — what so many have done for us that cost them their lives.'

Betty went to her father and kissed him on the cheek.

'Of course, Tom,' Herbie muttered. 'I'm not suggesting otherwise.'

'Actually, you were,' Peg interjected.

Betty silently blessed her. Peg, like her father, always said those things other people dare not. Betty only wished she could be as brave.

'I like your dad,' Ben whispered to Betty when she brought him another half pint of ale.

'So do I.'

'I had no idea we were so unwelcome here! I mean in Britain, not just in Midchester or this pub.'

'It's just that a lot of girls' heads have been turned by handsome Americans,' Betty explained. 'You all seem very glamorous to us, like cowboys or movie stars. And chocolate helps, of course!'

'I didn't know how far rationing had spread here till I arrived,' Ben said. 'In America we're not short of anything, because we produce most of our own food.'

'We're only a small island,' Betty explained. 'We rely a lot on imports and the ships just aren't getting through, for obvious reasons. Not that we're totally helpless. Everyone has an allotment for vegetables, and we keep a few animals. Some of us share in the rearing. In fact, we're having a pig roast next Saturday night. All are welcome to attend for the bargain price of half a shilling. That will help to buy another pig.'

'That sounds great. Maybe I'll come down, and bring some of the guys.'

'Don't bring too many,' Betty said, laughing. 'The pig might not go around the entire American military.'

'OK, I'll just bring my friend, Charlie Turner. It's about time he went out more. He's not injured. His problem is more psychological.'

'I'm sorry to hear that. Mrs Baker's father came back shell-shocked from the Great War.'

'It definitely gets to you after a while.'

Betty didn't know how to answer that, so she smiled sympathetically and moved away to wash up some glasses.

The pub was busier than ever, and Betty couldn't help wondering if the Stocking Stealer had something to do with that. It had certainly brought excitement to the village.

The war seemed a million miles away. The bombing raids happened in the big cities and towns. People listened to the wireless every evening for news, but even that added a certain distance to the events taking place, like listening to a radio play or watching a film.

So the Stocking Stealer was big news. Men argued over ways of dealing with the criminal, when he (or she) was found, whilst the women in the lounge were more interested in who it might be.

'I'm sure,' Myrtle Simpson said, 'that if men's socks were being stolen, the men would be trying harder to find the person, instead of just sitting there talking about what they're going to do when he's caught. Betty, dear, can I have another glass of lemonade, please?'

Betty gave Myrtle her lemonade.

'Have you heard anything about Eddie?' Myrtle asked in a low voice, as if it was a big secret that her son had been missing for two years.

'No, nothing. I'd tell you as soon as I did,' Betty said.

'Of course you would. I was only saying to Len last night that you are not like these other girls, chasing after all the Americans who come here. 'She's faithful to our Eddie's memory'. Not that I believe he's dead. Oh, no.'

Myrtle took her drink and went to sit with her friends. Before Betty could move away from the bar, Peg put her hand over Betty's.

'You've been faithful long enough, dear. It's time you started to live again, instead of burying yourself in Eddie's memory.'

'It's difficult, when . . . ' Betty floundered, because she did not want to speak ill of Eddie's parents. Of course they wanted their son to be alive and well, and she wished that for them. It was not knowing that made things so difficult.

'When they're reminding you all the time about having to be a good and faithful young woman?'

'Yes.'

'It's unfair of them, although I understand how they want to cling on to hope. But they shouldn't inflict that on you.'

'One day we might know for sure,' Betty said. 'Oh, that sounds awful. As if I'm wishing he were dead!'

'No-one would ever accuse you of that, dear.'

Betty realised that Ben was watching from the other side of the bar. She moved away and tried to look busy again. Something about him unnerved her. It was not an unpleasant feeling, but it was an unwelcome one, given her circumstances.

When she looked around again, some time later, Ben had gone. In fact, almost everyone had gone. Her father shooed out a few drinkers who always tried to flout the licensing laws by staying beyond closing time.

'Now we can eat,' he said, clapping his hands together.

'I made a pie out of the leftover

corned beef. And there are a few potatoes left from Sunday lunch. I'll fry them up, shall I, Dad?'

'That sounds grand, love. I'll clean up here and be up in about ten minutes.' He started clearing the tables.

'Betty . . . ' he added, before she left the bar.

'Yes, Dad?'

'I heard what Peg said to you. She's right, you know. It's time for you to start living again. When I lost your mother, I didn't think I'd ever love again. But now . . . '

'Maggie?' Betty smiled. Maggie was the barmaid who worked in the pub in the evenings.

'Yes. You don't mind, do you?'

'Of course not, Dad. It's what Mum would have wanted.'

'Well, then, I think that you living again is what Eddie would have wanted.'

Betty shook her head.

'I doubt it. He could be possessive, if you remember. That's why I feel stuck to this promise.'

'That promise would have been worth more if he'd offered you an engagement ring before he went.'

'Let's not go over this now, Dad, eh?'

'OK. But I'm here if you ever need to talk. I know I'm not your mum, and can't always talk about the same sort of things that women do, but I've tried my best with you.'

Betty lifted the flap on the bar and went into the saloon, throwing her arms around her father.

'You've done better than your best, Dad.'

'Be Yourself'

After they'd eaten their late lunch, Tom got on with changing the barrels in the cellar, whilst Betty went out for a walk to clear her head. It was spring in Midchester, and the trees were in blossom. She thought about the young men fighting hundreds of miles away and wondered if they ever had time to notice such beauty.

Her feet took her to the churchyard. She liked to look at the old gravestones and tend her mum's grave if it needed it. Sometimes she sat talking to her mum, sharing her problems. Not out loud. Even in the churchyard, such thoughts were not private — anyone could pass along the footpath and hear her. But Betty knew that, even when she didn't speak, her mum knew what she was saying.

She was just walking up the path

when she noticed a pair of long legs stretched out in the porch way. She knew it was Ben without needing to see the rest of him, but there was something about the position of the legs that worried her.

'Ben?' She hurried to the church porch. 'Are you all right?'

He was sitting on the bench, his face ashen gray and a thin veil of sweat lining his brow.

'I overdid the sightseeing,' he explained with a wry grin.

'I find that hard to believe, in Midchester.' Even while she joked, Betty was concerned about him. 'Do you need a doctor?'

'No, I just need to rest until I have the strength to walk back to the hospital.'

'Let me get Dad to help you. He could use the car.'

'I know gas is rationed here, Betty. Your father doesn't need to waste it taking me home, just because I was stupid enough to overdo it. I'll be fine. I just need time to recover.'

'Can I get you anything, then? A glass of water? Or are you sure you don't need the doctor?'

'If you really want to help, maybe you could lend me your shoulder to walk back to the hospital. If it's not taking you too far out of your way.'

'Of course not.' She sat down next to him. 'Rest awhile first. What happened to your legs, Ben? That is, I know you crashed, but what damage did it do?'

'Mostly surface damage, thankfully. I think it's just that, lying down for so long whilst they healed, my muscles have wasted a little. I used to run marathons when I was in college. Now, I can't get from the church gate to the porch!'

'I'm sure you'll get a medal for it soon.' Betty smiled.

'Do you often come walking in the graveyard?'

'Yes, most days.'

'Ah.'

'What?'

'I guess I hoped that you saw me here.'

'I don't make a habit of following young men,' Betty said stiffly.

And yet hadn't her heart flipped when she saw it was him in the porch? She pushed the thought aside.

'I didn't mean to offend you.'

'You didn't. Not really. It's just . . . '

'Tell me about Eddie.'

'Eddie?'

'Your sweetheart.'

'Why do you want to know?'

'He must be a pretty special guy to have such a beautiful girl waiting for him.'

'He's just Eddie, I suppose. I've known him since we were at primary school together here in Midchester. Peg Bradbourne was one of our teachers. It took me ages to be able to call her Peg when I left school and was old enough to help Dad in the pub. She was a great teacher, very inspirational. I thought I'd like to become a teacher myself, but the war happened, then Mum died. Dad needed me.'

'That's sad, but it doesn't tell me about you and Eddie. Are you ready to start helping me walk back now?'

'Of course,' Betty said, flustered. Now he would think that she didn't care about Eddie.

She helped Ben to his feet and they started walking steadily towards the gate at the back of the church, with him resting on her shoulder.

'This is a short cut to Bedlington Hall,' Betty explained. 'Some of it is cross-country, but it's solid ground, so you should be all right if you want to use this route again.'

'Thank you. This is my own fault. I was told to use a walking-stick, but my male pride wouldn't let me. Next time I'll know better.'

'I think a walking-stick gives a man a certain distinguished air,' Betty cajoled.

'Then I'll definitely use one next time! So, you were telling me about Eddie.'

'I thought you complained that I wasn't!'

'Now I'm asking again. Why are you avoiding it?'

'Can I be honest with you, Ben? That is, if I tell you the truth, will you promise not to think I'm a dreadful person?'

'I doubt anyone could think that about you.'

'Eddie and I, as I said, have known each other since childhood. Our parents used to joke that we would marry, because we were inseparable. He was a good friend. We used to go scrumping up at Bedlington farm together.'

'Scrumping?' He looked bemused.

'It means pinching apples from trees. Well, we sort of fell into going out together, because everyone expected it. Then the war came, and he asked me to promise I'd wait for him, to give him something to hope for whilst he was away. He asked me in front of my dad, his parents and the whole pub. What else could I say but yes?'

'It was the only thing you could do.'

'Eddie managed to survive Dunkirk, but even though he came back to Britain for a short time, he didn't come home. He went back to fight again, still without coming home. Then the telegraph came, saying he was missing in action. Since then his parents have longed for his return. I want him to come back, too. Only . . . '

'Only what?'

'Only I'm tired of having to act a certain way! If I smile too much or laugh too much, I feel guilty, because I know they're thinking of Eddie. If I dare to enjoy myself for a few minutes, I feel guilty. All my friends, those of my own age, have given up on me, because I've turned down so many invitations to go out with them.'

Betty hadn't realised she had begun to cry.

'Sometimes I would like to feel like a young girl again. I know it's selfish of me. Len and Myrtle have invested all their hopes and dreams in me. It's just a heavy burden to carry sometimes.'

Betty stopped, appalled. She had never even said all those things to her father.

'Oh, listen to me,' she said impatiently. 'Here I am, moaning about my lot, and you're the one who's been out there fighting, getting injured!'

'Whoever said that war was easy for those who stayed behind, Betty? Sometimes I think it can be harder. A good amount of the time, we're all safe behind some lines somewhere, waiting for the next order to move forward.

'But the folks back home don't know that, because we can't say where we are. My mom writes letters to me and her worries are etched in every line. I know she's going to keep on worrying, no matter how much I tell her I'm fine. Getting shot down hasn't helped!'

'I can imagine. And now I feel awful.'

'Stop feeling awful, Betty. There are no rules for how one should feel during war. Our world leaders tell us to be stoic and brave, but deep down we can only be ourselves.'

'I'm not even sure who myself is, Ben. I was nineteen when Eddie left for war, and he was twenty. I'd barely finished growing up before I made the promise to him.'

'You didn't get engaged?'

'Not really. It was sort of a promise to become engaged when he returned.'

Betty decided to change the subject.

'Tell me about New York, where you come from.'

'It's a big, noisy, dirty, busy, wonderful city. I was born and brought up in Brooklyn, and my dad is a cop. When the war is over, I intend to become a cop, too.'

'Like in the movies!'

'Like in the movies. We don't have much in New York City to rival these beautiful hills though.'

' "Those blue remembered hills . . . " '

'Excuse me?'

'It's part a poem by A. E. Housman, about Shropshire. It's rather sad really, about the loss of youth and how you can never walk the same path again. Even if it is the same path, you are different.'

It was a few minutes before she spoke again.

'We have a Roman fort, if you're interested in seeing it. There's not a lot of it. Archaeologists came before the war and took a lot of it away, but if you stand at the top of that hill . . . ' she pointed into the distance ' . . . you can see the earthworks and some of the wall that remains.'

'Maybe I'll do that, when my leg is stronger.'

'I meant later, when you're better.'

'When I'm better I'll be back off to war again.'

'Oh.'

'Let's not think of that now. Do you know what you need, Miss Betty Yeardley?'

Betty didn't bother to ask how he knew her surname.

'What do I need?' she said warily.

If he asked her to go out with him,

she would have to refuse. Except she did not want to.

'You need some excitement.'

'Oh,' she said, even more warily.

'Yes. Something to occupy your mind. I give to you the Secret of the Stolen Stockings.'

'What?' Betty burst out laughing.

'The Secret of the Stolen Stockings! You and I will set out on a quest to bring the sneak thief to justice, and reunite the ladies of Midchester with their stockings.'

'I can't go snooping on my neighbours!'

'There's no snooping involved. You just speak to people casually, and find out as much as you can about the thefts. Then you make a list of suspects. Come on — it'll be fun!'

'What if the thief is dangerous?'

'Then I don't think he or she would have stuck to stealing stockings.'

'But you said yourself that such things can escalate.'

'That's why I'm with you. With your

brains and beauty and my muscle (apart from the bad leg) we'll be perfect sleuths!'

'Whatever put this idea into your head, Ben?' Betty had to admit it sounded like fun.

'Not what. Who!'

'Peg Bradbourne?'

'Hey, you're good. How did you guess that so quickly?'

'Because Peg has a thing about sleuthing. She used to do a lot of it before the war started.'

'You're right, it was Peg. I saw her when she left the pub, and she said it would be a great way to, well, to get you out and about a little more.'

Betty suspected he was about to say something else, and wondered what it might be. She hoped Peg wasn't trying to do some matchmaking. She'd been known to do that. Several couples in Midchester had begun their relationship whilst helping Peg to track down some wrongdoer.

'I don't know,' she prevaricated,

becoming convinced that this was exactly what Peg was up to. 'I have to help Dad in the pub a few days a week, and evenings, and another couple of days a week I work on Bedlington Farm for the war effort.'

'That's perfect! You speak to people when they're in the pub, or when you see them on your way to the farm, or when you're out walking, like today. You must get time off sometimes. Mr Yeardley doesn't look like a slave-driver to me!'

'Of course he isn't. Dad's lovely.'

'Yep, I thought he was lovely, too.'

Betty laughed at that.

'You really are the limit, Ben.'

They were drawing nearer to the hospital. Betty could see several service-men sitting out under the veranda. Some, who were clearly becoming fitter, walked in the gardens.

'Hey, Ben!' A good-looking young man with sandy coloured hair broke away from a group of servicemen and strode across the grass. 'We were just wondering where you'd got to.' He stopped when he saw Betty. 'Oh, are there any more like you at home?'

'She's pretty unique, I'd say.' Ben shook his head. 'Betty, this rogue is my friend, Charlie Turner. Charlie, this is Miss Betty Yeardley, and I order you to be nice to her. She's a lady and not used to ruffians like yourself.'

Charlie took Betty's hand and kissed it.

'I shall be the perfect gentleman. My, you really are pretty.'

'Thank you.' Betty became shy. 'I really should get back, Ben. Are you OK now?'

'Yes, thanks.'

'Why? What happened?' One of the nurses, a pretty red-haired girl of about twenty-two, came forward. Her accent had a slight Scottish lilt to it.

'He overdid things a bit,' Betty said.

'Ben, we did warn you.'

'I know, Fiona, but I guess I thought I could manage the walk.'

'You obviously couldn't,' Fiona spoke

indignantly. 'I'm going to be telling the doctor to keep you in for a few days.'

'You can't do that. We have to catch the Sinister Stocking Stealer.'

'The what?' Charlie burst out laughing and Fiona smiled, but Betty saw something else in her eyes.

'There's someone stealing stockings in the village,' Betty explained, still watching Fiona.

'Here, too!' the young nurse said, confirming Betty's suspicions. 'Some of the girls have had theirs stolen from the laundry room. It's very inconvenient, not to mention expensive. At first we thought some of the patients were playing a practical joke. Honestly, there's no controlling them when they start to recover!'

She spoke with mock sternness but Betty could tell she had real affection for her charges.

'But they swear they haven't, and quite honestly, I believe them. They'd soon get bored with a joke like that, and they usually own up in the end. They get fun out of seeing our reactions when we realise we've been had.'

'The game is afoot!' Charlie raised a finger to the sky theatrically. 'We must find the Stocking Stealer before it's too late.'

'What's your definition of too late?' Betty asked, fearing what might happen next, and remembering Ben's words about crime escalating.

'Oh, I don't know.' Charlie spoke with a cheeky grin. 'About half past nine?'

Gossip And Lies

It was getting late, so Betty said her goodbyes to Ben, Charlie and Fiona and headed back along the path towards home. She felt happier than she had for a while. It had felt good to be amongst young people. Ben was charming, Charlie made her laugh and Fiona, behind her starched uniform, had a kind heart and ready wit.

She was nearing the churchyard when she saw Myrtle Simpson standing near the back gate with her arms folded and a grim expression on her face.

'Evening, Mrs Simpson,' Betty said as brightly as she could when she drew level with the lady.

'Good evening, Betty. Had a nice walk?'

'Yes, thanks. It's nice to get away from the pub.'

'Betty, I'm sure there's nothing to

worry about. You're a good girl, you always have been. But, well, it doesn't look good, running around with American airmen when Eddie is off fighting for his country. I'm sure there's nothing to it, and you're innocent of any wrongdoing . . . '

'Captain Greenwood had taken unwell!' Anger flared in her, but she managed to keep it in check. 'I just helped him to get back to Bedlington Hall.'

'Why didn't you ask your father to loan you the car?'

'Ben — Captain Greenwood — wouldn't hear of it. He understands that petrol is in short supply. Anyway, I'm back now, and I must get on. Dad will be waiting for me to help with the evening crowd.'

'I just wouldn't want Eddie to come home and get the wrong impression, that's all, Betty.'

'There is no impression for anyone to get, Mrs Simpson. I am allowed to speak to people of my own age, you know, even if they are of the opposite sex. It doesn't mean I'm taking up with them.'

Betty was trying to keep her temper. She understood Mrs Simpson's point of view. Her boy was missing in action, and that didn't mean that he would not be coming home. She clung to hope, as any mother would.

'If Eddie has a problem with that, when he returns, then he can take it up with me.' Betty tried to think of something to say to soften her words. 'I know it's hard for you, not knowing but . . . '

'That's why we have to keep that beacon of hope, Betty. That's why you have to remain faithful to him. So that none of us have anything to reproach ourselves for, when he comes home. I don't want him to think we've given up on him, you see.'

'I do see.' Betty put her hand on Mrs Simpson's arm. 'I understand. I really do. But you've nothing to worry about. Captain Greenwood is just a friend.'

'A friend?' Mrs Simpson's eyes

narrowed. 'You've only known him a few hours.'

'Well, let's just say he's done nothing to earn the title of enemy yet,' Betty said, her anger rising again.

If Mrs Simpson was determined to twist her every word, there was not much more she could do or say.

★ ★ ★

She flew through the pub door just as her father and Maggie Potter were setting things up for the evening shift.

'Are you all right, sweetheart?' her father asked. 'You look like you have got the four horsemen of the apocalypse behind you.'

'I'm fine, Dad. I'll just go and freshen up, and then I'll be back downstairs to help. Evening, Maggie.' Betty's voice softened.

Maggie was an attractive red-haired lady in her forties. She had lost her husband early in the war, so she had much in common with Tom.

'Evening, Betty. You sure you're all right, love?'

'Yes, I'm OK, really. That is . . . ' Betty shut the pub door and locked it securely. 'I've just had a run-in with Mrs Simpson. She's upset because I walked Ben back to Bedlington Hall. I told her there's nothing in it.'

'Ben?' Maggie raised an eyebrow.

'Captain Ben Greenwood.' Tom grinned as he lifted a chair off a table and put it on the floor. 'The handsome, American hero type who came in this afternoon. I told you about him.'

'Ah, that Ben!' Maggie smiled and winked.

'I was just helping an injured serviceman, that's all,' Betty said petulantly.

She rushed past them and upstairs, where she threw herself on her bed and beat her pillow with her hands in frustration.

Just a few minutes later, she felt a soft hand stroking her hair.

'I'm here, if you ever want to talk,

Betty,' Maggie said. 'I know I'm not your mum, and I don't want to take her place in any way, but I do understand what you're going through.'

'I like him, Maggie. I like him a lot.'

'Captain Ben?'

'Yes. Is that wrong of me? Don't answer that. I know it is, with Eddie missing. I'm just a dreadful person!'

'No, you're not. You're a kind, caring person. And you're also very young still. I know your father and Peg have already said this to you, Betty, but you can't put your life on hold for ever.'

'Mrs Simpson seems to think I should.'

'That's because hers is. It's bound to be. I was the same when my Arthur went missing, until I found out for certain. But you and Eddie weren't married — you weren't even engaged to be married. Even if he is still alive somewhere, you have to allow for the fact that four years changes people.'

'But if I really loved him, I would wait, wouldn't I? That's the worst thing,

Maggie. I wouldn't wish any harm come to Eddie, but I don't think I love him. I don't know if I ever did.'

Betty sat up and took a deep breath.

'But that doesn't justify breaking a promise.'

'A promise made when you were barely twenty years of age. Would you like me to have a word with Mrs Simpson? I could tell her to back off a little.'

'No, please don't. She's suffering so much, I don't want to make her unhappier still. If — when — Eddie comes back, maybe things can be sorted out. Until then, I have to keep my promise. It's for my own sake as well as hers, Maggie.'

'So, no Captain Ben?'

'No Captain Ben. But we can still be friends, can't we?' Betty filled Maggie in on the plans to find the Stocking Stealer.

'Hmm.'

Maggie pursed her lips.

'What does 'Hmm' mean?'

'It means that I can see someone getting her heart broken.'

'Not me. If I'm attracted to him, it's only because there are precious few young men around with them all off fighting the war, and he's the first good-looking man I've seen in a long time. That's all it is.'

They went downstairs to help Tom get ready for evening opening. Eventually people began to drift in from work, and the talk was of the Stocking Stealer as it had been at lunchtime.

After seven o'clock, Peg took up her seat at the bar in the ladies' lounge, whilst Mrs Simpson and her friends sat in the corner with their lemonade.

* * *

To Maggie's surprise, Ben, Charlie and Fiona arrived around eight o'clock.

'Ah, you made it,' Peg called before anyone else could say anything.

'We sure did, Miss Bradbourne,' Ben replied. 'We're very grateful to you for the use of your car.'

'Well, I hardly get out anywhere nowadays, so you might as well use my petrol rations.'

'Mr Yeardley,' Ben said, 'could we borrow Betty for a while?'

'It's Tom, and yes, you can borrow Betty.' Her father smiled.

'Just a minute,' Maggie interjected. 'Is no-one going to introduce me to the American hero?'

Betty blushed, whilst Tom made the introductions.

'And I'm the American hero's ugly friend,' Charlie Turner said. 'Lieutenant Charles Turner, at your service, ma'am.'

'Well, if you're what Americans call ugly, I'm emigrating tomorrow!'

Betty noticed Fiona looked a bit unhappy at that.

'And you must be Fiona. Betty said you were very pretty.' It was just like Maggie to notice, and put Fiona at her ease.

'Why don't you all go in the snug to talk? It'll be private in there.' Tom pointed to the small room at the side of the saloon. 'What can I get you all to drink?'

They ordered their drinks and went into the snug.

'Do we have snugs in America?' Charlie asked.

'I don't think so,' Ben told him.

'In that case, I'm writing to the President and demanding all American bars have them in future. *Snug*. I like that word!'

'So,' Ben said once they had their drinks, 'what have we got so far in the case of the Stocking Stealer?'

'I don't have anything,' Betty confessed. 'I'm sorry, I haven't had time to ask.'

'I didn't mean that. I just meant, what do we have so far?' He produced a tiny notebook and pencil from his top pocket. 'We need to list everyone who's had their stockings stolen so we can question them.'

'They took mine this afternoon!' Charlie offered.

'Hey, Doctor Watson.' Fiona playfully punched Charlie's arm. 'If you're not going to be serious, then you're off the case.'

'I'm sorry, Miss Sherlock Holmes. I'm just so excited to be sitting in a snug. In Britain. It wasn't on my list of dreams, and now I'm wondering why.'

'While you sit here and think about being in a snug, we'll get on with the hard work.' Ben rolled his eyes heavenward.

'There was Peg Bradbourne,' Betty began. 'Hers were taken this morning. Peg lives in the Old Constable's house, down next to the railway station. Then Mrs Baker's were taken. She lives near there.'

Ben made a list as Betty gave him all the names.

'Oh, and Maggie, our barmaid, had hers taken, too. About a week ago.'

Fiona joined in with a list of girls at Bedlington Hall who'd lost theirs.

'All in broad daylight. It doesn't make sense.'

46

'No, it doesn't,' Betty agreed. 'We'd know if there was a stranger about, so it must be someone local. But why? If it was someone who needed them, because they were poor or something, people in Midchester would help them out. We look after our own here.'

'It wasn't just stockings.' Maggie was washing glasses on the other side of the bar. 'Some chocolate, too. Taken from my pantry.'

'When was this?'

'The other day. Sorry, I forgot to mention it. I got given it from one of the airmen at the base, in return for some eggs from my chickens. He said he was fed up of dried eggs. I can't say I blame him — awful things, they are.'

'A pint, please, Maggie,' Herbie Potter called. 'When you've a minute.'

'Of course, Herbie.' Maggie bustled away. 'You all right, love? How's Floss, by the way?'

'She's fine. Still with her sister, Mildred, in Wales. You did know Mildred lost her husband?'

'Yes, you said. Such a pity. Why don't you come over to mine for dinner tomorrow?'

'I don't need charity, Maggie.'

'I'm your big sister, Herb. That doesn't count as charity. Honestly, men!'

'What are that lot up to?' Herbie gestured towards the snug.

'They're playing at being sleuths. I just told them, I had some chocolate taken as well. Unless I ate it, and forgot!' Maggie laughed.

'They ought to be off fighting in the war. The young men, at least. It's not a game when things go missing.' Herbie Potter sniffed and took his pint back to his seat.

'So, chocolate and stockings,' Ben was saying. 'That's suggestive, isn't it?'

'We're looking for someone with a sweet tooth and great legs?' Charlie suggested.

Ben swiped him with the notepad.

'No, idiot!' He paused and looked at the two ladies. 'How can I put this

48

politely? They're . . . '

'The currency of love?' Betty supplied. 'They're what American airmen give to the girls they like.'

'Yeah, I guess you could call it that.'

'Unless it's someone who's cold and hungry,' Fiona said.

'But if it's to do with needing food, surely they'd be more likely to steal Maggie's eggs,' Betty reasoned. 'Not her chocolate!'

'They might have taken eggs as well,' Ben said. 'After all, no-one knows exactly how many eggs a chicken lays each morning.'

'That's a dreadful thing to do, especially in wartime.' Betty frowned. 'Are you thinking it might be someone with a grudge against the American servicemen, Ben?'

'That's what's on my mind.'

'But I can't imagine who. There have been some romances in Midchester, but obviously Peg doesn't run around with Americans, nor does Maggie.'

Betty picked up the glasses almost

automatically and went back to the bar. She could see her father in deep conversation with Len Simpson. Used to being able to tune out the pub noises, she could just make out what they were saying.

'We're only saying, Tom . . . '

'I know what you're saying, Len. I'm asking you to cut my daughter some slack. She's young, for goodness' sake. She can't live like a nun.'

'What if our Eddie walked in tonight, eh? How do you think he'd feel?'

'I hope he would know that Betty is a good girl, and understand that she can't live her life in suspended animation until he returns. She's doing no wrong, Len.'

'Well I'm sure you'd say so, running around with Maggie when your wife and her husband are barely cold in the grave!'

Betty gasped. That was a dreadful thing to say! She knew for a fact that her father and Maggie had only been in a relationship for a few months.

'Len?' Tom replied in a level voice, but Betty knew her father well enough to be certain that he was very angry indeed. 'I don't want to ban you from my pub, but any more talk like that and you'll be out. Do you understand? I don't have to justify myself to you, or anyone else, and I won't have you disrespecting Maggie. She's a good, decent woman.'

'I . . . well, sorry, Tom. Of course she is.' Len looked down at his feet. 'It's just — these Americans, coming over here, stealing all the girls, turning their heads with silk stockings and chocolate.'

'My Betty is not the sort of girl to be impressed by such trifles.'

'Are you OK, Dad?' Betty asked when her father came over to the snug side of the bar.

'I'm fine, sweetheart.' He reached across the bar and cupped her face in his hand. 'If you have the chance to be happy in this crazy, mixed-up, bombed-out world, my angel, you grab that chance with both hands.'

Her hands were trembling when she took the drinks back the table. She felt as though she was being pulled in two directions, and that on either side lay pain and heartache.

If the Simpsons and others were gossiping about her father and Maggie, what might they say about her, if she broke her promise to Eddie? Living and working in the pub, which was the main meeting place for villagers, she knew well how people gossiped. She hated the idea of being the subject of some of the whispering in the corner tables.

On The Trail

'Where shall we start?' Fiona asked. It was the next morning and the four young people stood in the middle of the village. The sky was bright above them, and as usual, when standing in the square, Betty found it hard to believe that a war was raging across the channel.

'First of all,' Ben said, 'I think we should split up. Fiona and Charlie, you take one half of the list. Betty and I will take the other half.'

'But we're strangers to everyone around here,' Fiona warned. 'Betty knows everyone.'

'That's true,' Betty agreed. 'They might not like strangers asking questions.'

'They're going to like it even less if four people turn up asking questions,' Ben explained. 'It would look a bit intimidating.'

'You're probably right.' Betty nodded. 'Whatever we're doing, we ought to get on with it. I promised Dad I'd be back by opening time. I've only got a couple of hours.'

'That settles it.' Ben clapped his hands together. 'Fiona and Charlie, you talk to everyone you see on the street, while Betty and I will knock on doors. She's known to the villagers, so it won't seem as intrusive. Make a list of everything that's gone missing, and who lost it.'

'Do you think there may be more thefts we don't know about?'

'It's possible.'

'I'm sure the constable would have heard about it.'

'I don't know, Betty. I notice you Brits are pretty stoic about things. With the war on, people don't want to complain, figuring there are more important things to worry about than a few petty thefts. Where do you think we should start?'

'Peg Bradbourne. She knows every-thing. In fact,' Betty said with a smile, 'we may find that Peg will tell us everything we need to know. She doesn't miss a thing.'

After saying farewell to Charlie and Fiona, Betty and Ben walked to the Old Constable's house, where Peg lived. It had not been a constable's house for many years, yet, in the way of old villages, it was still called that. It was a rambling old house, full of character, with some parts of it very old, and some new extensions that had been added in the past twenty years.

'It used to have a gaol attached,' Betty explained to Ben as they drew near. 'I think it's the pantry now.'

'Where do the prisoners go?'

'They take them to the big towns. I can't imagine Peg would be happy if they were kept in her larder, do you?'

Betty knocked on the door and they heard Peg call on them to come in.

'Well, this is a nice surprise,' Peg said when they entered her cosy sitting-room. 'I saw you coming this way, and I put the kettle on, hoping you'd call in.'

'I have a gift for you,' Ben said. 'But you must promise not to take it the wrong way.'

He slipped his hand into his inside pocket and drew out a pair of stockings, still in their wrapper.

Peg laughed as she took them from him.

'Thank you, kind sir. Now, sit down, both of you, and tell me what you've been doing.'

'Nothing yet.' Betty took a seat on a chair near to the fireplace, and felt disconcerted when Ben sat on the arm, rather than sitting on the sofa. 'You're our first witness.'

'A witness?' Peg laughed. 'Not a suspect? I am disappointed.'

She went to make the tea. Still disturbed by Ben's proximity, Betty got up and pretended to look at pictures on the fireplace.

'That's Peg's niece, Meredith,' she explained, showing a picture of a toothy, freckle-faced young girl with flaming auburn locks. 'She lives near

Sheffield with her other aunt, Peg's sister. And look, here are some old pictures of when this was the constable's cottage. Apparently one constable in Victorian times was called Hounds. That's a very apt name for a policeman, isn't it? He arrested Peg's great-grandfather, who was a doctor, on suspicion of murder, but luckily the real killer was found by Peg's great-grandmother. So sleuthing runs in her veins!'

'They sound like a very tenacious family.'

'You have no idea. Nothing gets past Peg. I wouldn't be surprised if she worked this out all on her own. She just seems to like involving others. She says it brings people together.'

Remembering that what Peg usually did was bring people together romantically, Betty became flustered, and fell into silence.

'Did Peg never marry?'

'No.' Betty lowered her voice. 'There's a rumour she fell in love with someone as a young woman, but they couldn't be together. She doesn't talk about it.'

'That's sad. It's probably why she likes to bring others together.'

'Perhaps.'

After browsing a bit longer, Betty went to the sofa and sat down.

'This cottage is wonderful.' Ben stood up from the arm of the chair and sat right down next to Betty on the sofa. His weight on the old springs caused them both to sink into the settee. 'The sort of place I dream of living in.'

'Don't you have places like this in New York?'

Ben shook his head.

'It's a city, with buildings built close together and no room to breathe. It's a wonderful city, but still busy. In America we like new things. A cottage like this would be knocked down and replaced with something more modern.'

'That's rather sad.'

Betty shuffled along the sofa a bit,

still feeling that Ben was too close for her liking. He made her heart beat much faster than it should have.

'What's rather sad?' Peg was carrying a tray full of tea things into the room.

'Ben said that they don't keep cottages like this in America. They like modern things better.'

'Goodness. Where do you keep all your ghosts?'

'Is this place haunted?' Ben looked amused and delighted.

'Of course it is. So is the pub.'

'Don't tell Maggie that,' Betty warned. 'Dad can hardly persuade her to go down in the cellar as it is.'

'What ghosts do you have in the pub?' Ben urged.

'They say that there used to be a tunnel, all the way from the sea,' Betty told him. 'And that smugglers used to come along there. The story goes that the local authorities decided to seal it up this end, and that a man got trapped down there.'

'Couldn't he have walked back the

way he came?' Ben raised a quizzical eyebrow.

'Now, where's the drama in that?' Peg said. 'Tea, Ben?'

'Yes, please, Miss Bradbourne.'

'Peg. I insist on being on first name terms with men who bring me stockings.' She winked.

'Talking of stockings,' Betty interrupted, realising they were in danger of forgetting why they were there. 'We're actually here to ask you about the theft of yours. Ben wonders if anything else has gone missing too. Did you know that Maggie had a bar of chocolate stolen?'

'Yes, I heard her mention it last night in the pub. As far as I know, nothing like that has gone missing from my stores. I can have a look, but with so little in there, due to rationing, I think I'd notice immediately if anything disappeared. And I'm not alone in that. Most of us would, nowadays.'

Ben took out his notepad. It made Betty want to laugh. He seemed to be taking it all very seriously indeed.

'Tell us about the morning your stockings went missing, Peg.' He looked from Betty to Peg, and it was then that she saw the twinkle in his blue eyes.

'As I told Betty the other day, it was just a normal morning. I got up early to do the washing and put it out on the line. Then I started on my other chores. The post came so I opened that. I'm always afraid that my sister and niece will come to harm over in Sheffield, but they have to stay there because my sister's husband does important work.' Her brow furrowed. 'Now, what else did I do? That was about it, really. It was just before I went to the pub that I checked on the washing to see if it were nearly dry, and saw that my stockings had gone missing.'

'Did you see anyone hanging around?'

'No, dear. Apart from the usual people one sees in the morning — the postman, the milkman, the ARP wardens going home from their night shift. I would have noticed. Strangers tend to stand out in Midchester. In fact, I saw you when you were on your way down from the hospital, just before I went into the pub.'

'I didn't steal your stockings, Peg.'

'Well, no, dear, they were already gone by then. Unless it was a double bluff on your part, and you only looked as if you were coming from the hospital but had in fact been in the area all along. I hear that stockings have gone missing from the laundry up there.'

Betty burst out laughing and shook her head at Peg.

'She's teasing you, Ben.'

'I hope so! I was getting kind of worried.'

'Peg, you've done some sleuthing in your time. You must have an idea of who is doing this!'

'I'm afraid I don't, dear. I've been racking my brains. Of course, in a case like this everyone is a suspect. What we're lacking is a motive, and no-one in Midchester, as far as I can tell, has a reason for stealing stockings and chocolate.'

'It could be children,' Betty suggested. 'They might take the stockings for a dare, and then the chocolate simply because there's not much of it around.'

'That's possible.' Peg nodded. 'There are a lot of evacuees who came here from the cities. That's not to say that local children aren't capable of mischief. But I don't feel it is children.'

'What makes you say that?'

'What do you Americans call it in those gangster movies?' she asked. 'A hunch?'

'That's what my dad would call it. He's a cop in New York.'

'How romantic,' Peg declared. 'Does he hunt down gangsters?' Her eyes sparkled.

'Not as far as I know. In his district it's mostly petty theft. Brooklyn may be part of a big city, but really it's as much a village as Midchester.'

'It must be exciting, having a

policeman as a father.'

'It can be, but Mom worries about him.'

'Tell us about your family, Ben,' Peg said.

'There's not much to tell. My great-grandfather emigrated from Germany in the late nineteenth century. Our real name is Grunewald but it was changed to Greenwood soon after he emigrated. My great-grandfather and grandfather were bakers. They wanted Dad to follow the family tradition, but he always wanted to be a cop. Mom is a schoolteacher, and her family emigrated from Italy at the turn of the century.'

'That explains your lovely, thick black hair,' Peg said. 'Don't you think his hair is lovely, Betty?'

'It's very nice,' Betty said primly.

'You and Betty have a lot in common. Betty's mother was from Italian stock, wasn't she, Betty?'

'Yes, she was.'

'In fact, Betty is actually Elisabetta, but she doesn't like to be called that.'

'Why not?' Ben turned to her. 'It's a beautiful name.'

'We're getting off the subject,' Betty said. 'If you've nothing else to tell us, Peg, we really ought to be going. I have to be back at the pub before eleven.'

'Oh, and just as things were becoming interesting.' Peg sighed. 'Very well, off you both go and catch our culprit — or culprits. Are you coming to the pig roast on Saturday, Ben?'

'I sure am.'

'Then if I don't see you before, I shall see you there.'

Ben and Betty walked out into the sunshine.

'We'll call in on Mrs Baker,' Betty decided. 'She's only next door to Peg.'

★ ★ ★

They found Mrs Baker in the garden, hanging out washing. She was only in her thirties, but bringing up five children alone had given her a frazzled air, making her look older than her

65

years. She worked as a cleaner at the hospital, but that did not pay very well, and she gave every impression of living on the breadline.

'What can I do for you?' she asked, as she pegged a rather grubby-looking sheet on the line.

'We're investigating the case of the missing stockings, Mrs Baker.' Betty smiled warmly. 'Peg Bradbourne said you'd had some taken.'

'Yes, that's right. But I know why you're really here. Well, you can just go back to that collection of crows in the pub and tell them I haven't stolen their stockings or their chocolate! I know what people think around here, because I'm on my own with the children. I admit they sometimes run riot. It's hard to keep track of five. But they're good children, and I won't have anyone say otherwise.' She jerked her head to take in the whole village. 'Just because we're poor doesn't mean we can't be honest.'

'No, it doesn't,' Ben agreed sympathetically.

'Can you tell us about the day your stockings went missing?' Betty asked, unsure if she liked the way Mrs Baker was looking Ben up and down.

Not that it was any of her business. But she couldn't help noticing that, close up, Mrs Baker was quite attractive. Her face had a good bone structure and her eyes were a pretty shade of hazel. Only the dark lines of tiredness under her eyes marred her features.

'There's not much to tell. I hung the washing out the afternoon before, thinking I'd bring it in before it got dark, but I was busy with the children, so forgot all about it. When I went out to check it the next morning, the stockings were gone. I noticed because they were my only pair.'

'So you couldn't really say if they disappeared on the afternoon you put them out, during the night or in the morning?'

'No.' Mrs. Baker started to shake her head. 'Hang on, though. Yes, I can! I came outside at around seven in the morning to bring in the milk. They were there then, because the washing had got all twisted up so I had to straighten it. The stockings were in a right mess. It had rained quite a bit during the night so I had to leave the washing out longer. That gave the neighbours something to talk about, I can tell you. It was when I went back later at ten that I noticed the stockings gone.'

'So they disappeared in the three hours between seven and ten?'

'Yes, that would be it. It's amazing what you remember when you have time to think about it.'

Mrs. Baker's attention was taking by something or someone beyond Betty and Ben.

'Good morning, Herbie. Have you got anything for me this morning?'

Betty turned to see Herbie Potter walking through a gap in the hedge between Peg's and Mrs Baker's.

'Only bills, I think,' Herbie said,

handing her the post. 'Morning, Betty, morning, Captain Greenwood,' he added curtly. 'Still investigating?'

'Yes. But we're not getting anywhere.'

'Well, you won't, if you go around accusing people, will you?'

'We're not accusing anyone, Mr. Potter,' Betty fired back. 'We're just asking questions. Actually, while you're here, we can ask you. Have you seen anything strange on your rounds? Or have you had anything stolen?'

'The only things I've seen are these young whippersnappers from the hospital running around. Seems to me that, if they're fit enough to walk to the pub and go around the village asking questions, they're fit enough to go back into combat.'

'Yes, you'd give Hitler what for, if not for your bad feet, wouldn't you, Herbie?' Mrs Baker commented pointedly.

'Yes, I would!' Herbie's cheeks became red. 'And I do my bit here for the Home Guard. You'd be worried if all the men were off fighting, leaving you ladies unattended.'

'Mr Potter,' Ben said, 'it would really help if you could tell us if anything had been stolen from you.'

'I'll check, but what with working on the post and doing my Home Guard duties, I don't have the luxury of checking my belongings every night.'

'We'll take that as a no, then.' Ben grinned.

'Honestly, Herbie Potter,' Mrs Baker said hotly. 'If it's not happening to you, it's not happening, is that it?'

'I didn't mean that.' Herbie looked taken aback.

'Well, I'm very happy for you that you have so many belongings that you don't care if any of them have gone missing. But I'm a widow bringing up five children on a paltry widow's pension and what I earn at the hospital. I can't afford to lose anything, for fear I'd have to replace it again. Stockings are one thing, but I worry myself sick every time the children need new clothes. What if someone starts stealing those off the line?'

'I didn't mean to offend you, Martha,' Herbie said. It was the first time Betty had heard Mrs Baker referred to by her first name.

'It isn't me you've offended, it's these nice young people who are trying to find out who the thief is. It's more than anyone else around here is doing.'

'Well, I've had nothing stolen, so that's that. If it happens, I'll let you know.'

'Thank you,' Betty said with a tight smile.

'Come on, Betty,' Ben told her. 'It's nearly eleven. Time for a glass of your best ale, I think! Why don't you join us, Mrs Baker? Take a few moments out from your hard work?'

'I can imagine what this lot would say about me if I went into the pub at lunch time. At any time, actually!'

'But you will come to the pig roast on Saturday, won't you?' Betty asked.

'I . . . er . . . no. It's not for me.'

Betty did a quick tot-up in her head, and realised that if Mrs Baker wanted to bring all her children it would be expensive for her. She wouldn't have that money to spare.

'You know,' Betty offered, 'we always get really busy in the pub. Perhaps you could come and help out — wash glasses, and what have you. You'd get free admission, and so would the children, because you're helping.'

That wasn't strictly true, but Betty would discuss it with her father. She was sure he would fix it so that Mrs Baker and her children could have a nice time.

'I suppose I could do that, for a few hours. It'd be nice to get out of the house.'

★ ★ ★

'That was kind,' Ben said as he and Betty walked back towards the village square.

'What was?'

72

'Finding a way that she could attend the pig roast and still keep her pride.' He reached into his pocket and took out a ten-shilling note. 'Here, this will cover their entry fee and mine.'

'You don't have to . . . '

'Betty, I've nothing to spend my money on here apart from your dad's pub, whereas I'm sure you and your dad can't really afford to give away free tickets. At least, not if you want to buy another pig. Take it, and don't argue.'

'OK.' Betty took the note and put it in her pocket. 'But it's still too much. I'll give you change when we get back to the pub.'

'No, you won't. Call it my contribution to the next pig roast. I might not be here for that, so maybe it'll make you think of me.'

'Are you returning to the war soon?' Betty felt an icy hand grip her heart.

'It won't be long. As soon as the docs here say I'm fit enough.'

'Oh.'

They had reached the village square.

Fiona and Charlie were on the bench, but Charlie looked deathly pale. He sat, muttering to himself, hugging his arms around him and rocking slightly.

'What's up?' Ben asked.

'Charlie has had one of his turns,' Fiona told them.

'You didn't need to wait for us. You should have taken him straight back to the hospital.'

'I can't.' She pointed to the car which was parked at the bottom of the square. 'Peg's car won't start. I don't know anything about cars, and Charlie was too poorly to help. I would have fetched your dad, Betty, but I was afraid to leave Charlie, and I don't think he could have made it to the pub.'

Ben made his way over to the car, leaving Betty, Fiona and Charlie by the bench.

Betty was used to seeing Charlie laughing and joking, but now he looked desperately sad, and his hands were trembling. She wanted to ask him if he was OK, but that seemed a silly question when he so obviously was not.

Ben had mentioned that Charlie's problems were psychological. She knew little about the brain, but if his stricken expression was anything to go by, she would have hated to be inside his head at that moment in time.

'Betty! Fiona!' Ben called them from the car, where he had the bonnet open.

'What is it?'

Betty had never seen Ben looking as serious as he did in that moment.

He wiped his forehead with an oil stained hand, leaving a streak of black across his head.

'Someone has stolen the rotor arm.'

Bravery

'Someone must have seen something.' Ben was leaning on the bar with a full glass of ale in front of him. He had been nursing it for a good ten minutes, but could not seem to bring himself to drink.

One of the villagers had taken Charlie and Fiona back to the hospital in his car, but Ben had elected to stay behind and ask questions.

The pub had not filled up with the lunchtime crowd yet, so there was just Betty, Ben, Maggie — who had come in to help out at a moment's notice — and Peg, who had come down to see what all the fuss was about.

Tom was at the garage, dealing with the car repairs on Peg's behalf. Ben and Charlie had insisted on paying for the repairs between them, despite Peg's protestations.

'The square is very quiet at that time of morning,' Maggie commented. 'In fact, it's very quiet most of the time.'

'At the bottom of the square, where Fiona parked,' Peg agreed, 'there's hardly anyone around. Few people drive in Midchester. The women walk to the shops, which are on the top road anyway, and most of the men walk to work much earlier in the morning. Apart from the almshouses at the bottom, that road sees hardly any traffic at all.'

'Someone in the almshouses might have seen something,' Betty suggested.

'That's possible,' Peg said. 'Old Mrs Mullins is always at her window. Do you want me to ask her when I go past on the way home?'

'Yes, thanks,' Betty replied.

'Maybe Betty and I could go.' Ben was suddenly alert. 'When the pub closes.'

'Oh, yes, that would be better.' Peg gave Maggie a secretive smile. 'Mrs Mullins was telling me only the other day that she had yet to meet a real live American. She doesn't manage to get out much, what with her bad legs, so she does miss a lot of what goes on in the village. That's probably why she sits in her window so much.'

'That's settled, then.'

'I haven't agreed yet,' Betty protested.

'I'm sorry, Betty.' Ben looked embarrassed. 'I only thought you'd want to be there. I can hardly go knocking at Mrs. Mullins's door alone. We could go tomorrow, if you're busy this afternoon.'

Betty shook her head.

'It's my day to help out up at Bedlington Farm. They've some new land army girls, and the farm manager says they're a bit silly and flighty at the moment. I have to go and frown at them sternly, or something!'

'Stern? I've never seen you looking anything but sweet.'

'Then you don't know me at all!'

To Betty's consternation, everyone

laughed at that. She supposed she was not very good at being stern. But she was determined to show those land girls that they could not mess around when there was a war on.

News of the missing rotor arm had spread, making it the main topic of conversation in the pub that lunchtime.

'First stockings and chocolate, now car parts! What is going on?' Len Simpson grumbled. 'And stealing from our own — that's all wrong. Has your father spoken to Constable Fisher about this, Betty?'

'I don't know.'

'Well, he ought to. And you and this young man need to stop playing detectives. This is serious now.'

'I like that!' Peg cried. 'When it was ladies' stockings and chocolate it wasn't worth bothering the constable with.' Betty stopped herself from reminding Peg that she was the one who hadn't wanted to bother the constable. 'Now it's a part from a car and it puts men's vehicles in danger, suddenly it's serious.

None of us can afford to lose anything, Len. We're not rich in Midchester.'

'I'm not saying otherwise. I'm only pointing out that the crime has done what this young man said it would do. It has escalated.'

They all started talking amongst themselves again.

At around one, after her father had returned, Professor Solomon turned up at the pub with his daughter, Rachel. He was in his sixties, but sprightly. Rachel was a plain woman in her forties, utterly devoted to her father. They went everywhere together.

'Hello, Professor Solomon, Miss Solomon,' Maggie said. 'We don't often see you in here.'

'Digging is thirsty work,' the professor said with a smile. 'Could we have a glass of lemonade each, please?'

'Of course.' Betty poured their drinks. 'How is the dig going? Have you found any Roman coins yet?'

'What's that about Roman coins?' Ben said from his seat at the bar.

'Professor, this is Captain Ben Greenwood. Ben, this is Professor and Miss Solomon. The professor is working up at the old Roman fort I told you about.'

'That's fascinating! I studied a bit of archaeology in college. Maybe I could talk to you about it sometime.'

'I'd be very happy to, Captain. In fact, I'm giving a talk on Monday evening at the village hall. I have slides to show of our finds so far.'

'I'll definitely be there — if they haven't shipped me back off by then.'

'It will be nice to have someone who shows a real interest.' The professor sighed. 'It will be nice to have someone there at all!'

'I would come, but I'm working here,' Betty apologised. 'Perhaps I could see the pictures another time, if you wouldn't mind.'

'Not at all, Betty. I know you have an interest in Midchester's past.'

Just then her father came up from the cellar, and Maggie took him aside and whispered to him.

'Betty,' he said, when they had finished. 'Maggie tells me you'd like to go to the professor's talk on Monday night.'

'Well, I just said I'd go if I didn't have to work.'

'You don't have to work. Maggie and I can cope on a Monday when it's quiet. Ben, you'll see she gets home safe, won't you?'

'I sure will, Tom.' Ben's face was alight.

Betty could feel a little bit of annoyance that people had started organising her life for her. For the rest of the evening, she kept repeating to herself that it was not a date with Ben. They just happened to be going to the same talk on archaeology!

It would probably be very dull. Such things often were. Nevertheless, whenever Betty had a chance to talk to the professor about his work, she had been fascinated with what he had to say.

Whether she would be able to

concentrate with Ben sitting beside her was another matter.

She went out into the bar to collect glasses, and saw Mr Simpson looking at her with a grim expression on his face. Deftly, she managed to get past him, in case he stopped her. Escaping Mrs Simpson in the ladies' lounge was harder, as it was not so busy, but she did her best to keep her head down as she collected glasses.

'Betty, can I have a word, please?'

'Not now, Mrs Simpson. I'm very busy.'

Mrs Simpson stood up and put her arm on Betty's.

'Someone saw that young man give you money today.'

Betty's face flared scarlet.

'It was his admission for the pig roast. I can't imagine what else anyone would think it was for.'

'Yes, I'm sure it was, dear. But I did tell you that people talk. If I know about it, so does everyone else.'

'Then everyone else can ask me

about it, and I'll tell them the same.'

'Now, Betty, don't get angry. You're a good girl.'

'So you keep telling me, Mrs Simpson, yet you don't really seem to believe it.'

Mrs Simpson looked surprised by Betty's vehemence. She stepped back a bit.

'Of course I believe you're a good girl, Betty. Just as I know you'll keep your promise to my Eddie.' She dabbed her eyes with her handkerchief. 'But you don't have a mother to watch over you, and what with you being Eddie's best girl, I feel as if I'm meant to take that place. I'm sure that as soon as he returns, I'll be your real mother — well, mother-in-law. I'm just taking care of you as he would want me to.'

'Thank you for that.' Betty's lips were set in a thin line. 'But I can take care of myself, and I don't need another mother!'

She slammed the glasses down on the bar, and dashed through the door leading to the pub's private rooms. She knew Mrs Simpson wouldn't follow her through there, as no-one, except Maggie who was practically family, entered the pub's private quarters without a personal invitation.

Betty went upstairs to the bathroom and swilled her hot face with cold water, looking at her burning cheeks in the mirror. She already felt guilty about the way she had spoken to Mrs Simpson, and knew she would have to apologise.

She wished she was as brave as her father. She knew him as a gentle, kind man, but running the pub for so many years had also given him a tough streak. He had no choice, if he was to deal with people who sometimes had a bit too much to drink. As a result, the customers respected him and knew better than to get in his bad books. Betty's mother, also kind and gentle with a smile that could melt an iceberg, had had a backbone of steel. Betty worried too much about whether people liked her or not, and it was this fear that made her feel guilty if she overstepped the mark.

She had been standing in front of the mirror for a moment or two when there was a knock on the bathroom door.

'Are you OK, love? We could use your help downstairs.'

'Yes, Dad. I'm coming now.'

She opened the door and saw her father standing there with a concerned expression on her face.

'Sorry, Dad. I think I was a bit rude to Mrs. Simpson.'

'She'll get over it.'

'Will she?'

'Sweetheart, you'd be surprised at some of the things I've said to customers. Yet they still come back.' He smiled wryly. 'We're the only pub in the village, so they have no choice, really.'

'People respect you, Dad.'

'They respect you, too. You have to stop being so apologetic all the time, sweetheart.'

'I don't like to think I've hurt anyone.'

'Did Mrs Simpson hurt you, when she made insinuations about Ben giving you that money?'

It didn't surprise Betty that her father knew exactly what had taken place. Not much happened in the pub without Tom knowing about it.

'Yes, she did.'

'Yet you're the one who feels you should say sorry?'

'She is older than me, dad. You always brought me up to respect my elders.'

'Betty, this pub has been in the family for three generations. I hope you'll take over when I'm gone.'

'Don't talk like that, Dad.'

'I'm not planning on going anywhere yet.' Tom smiled. 'I'm only talking in terms of retiring. But if you are going to take over — if you want to, that is — you're going to have to learn to be tougher with people. When they've had a drink they say lots of silly things, and you must learn not to let it bother you.'

'Mrs Simpson wasn't drunk.'

'That makes what she said even more unforgivable. Come on, put that lovely smile back on your face. Show that you're not bothered about what she says.'

Betty started to follow him down the stairs.

'Dad?'

'What, sweetheart?'

'I don't think I should go to the professor's talk on Monday night.'

Tom sighed.

'That's up to you, Betty.'

'You're angry with me.'

'No, never that. I just wish . . . ' He sighed again. 'If the truth be known, sometimes I wish I'd encouraged you to go away to join the land army or join one of the services, to broaden your horizons. Then you might see that those things you worry so much about, like small-town gossip, mean nothing in the bigger, wider world. I've been selfish, keeping you here since your mum died.'

'Dad, you're the least selfish person I know. And I'd never have gone away and left you.'

She took a deep breath and followed her father back into the bar. If Mrs Simpson looked at her, she made a point of not looking back. She fixed a smile on her face instead and went about her business.

Realising she would have to tell Ben about not going to the professor's talk, she went to look for him. He was not at his usual seat and was nowhere else to be seen in the pub.

'I saw Len having words with him,' Maggie said in low tones. 'He left soon after.'

She wanted to ask Len Simpson what he had said, but dared not. Perhaps it would be better if Ben had been put off spending time with her. It would make her life easier if he kept away.

That was what she told herself as she fixed her smile back in place and went about her work. In reality, her heart was heavy and she would be sad not to see his smile one last time before the pub closed after lunch.

Ben didn't return that afternoon either, so the visit to Mrs Mullins did not take place. Betty felt too shy about going alone.

She spent a miserable afternoon trying to read a book before the pub opened again, resisting the urge to go for a walk in the hopes of finding him in the churchyard. She hoped he might return that night, but there was no sign of him then either.

A couple of times she went to the door of the pub, and looked out, hoping to see him coming down the road. As it was starting to stay light later into the evenings, they did not have to worry about the blackout till around nine o'clock.

When it seemed certain he would not come, she resigned herself to the fact that Mr Simpson had frightened him off. Part of her regretted that, and wished that Ben had been more courageous.

She chastised herself for that thought, knowing that she had also been determined to put Ben off.

That had obviously worked, so why she felt as if her heart would break in two when the pub closed that night and she still had not seen him, she did not know.

The Terrible Twins

It was late by the time Betty got to bed, and she had to be up very early the next morning. The last customers left at eleven, and it took Betty, Tom and Maggie till nearly midnight to clear everything away. Tom walked Maggie home, as he did every night.

When Betty's alarm clock went off at six the next morning, she groaned, wishing she could have another hour in bed. It was one of her days for helping on Bedlington Farm, so she got up and put on her short-sleeved shirt, bib-and-brace overalls and a green pullover. She finished it with a hat. It was the uniform worn by the regular Land Army Girls. Betty could have been called up, but her mum's death had given her a reprieve. However, she still liked to help when she could.

After a quick breakfast of porridge, Betty packed up a slice of bread and jam and started the walk up to Bedlington Farm. It was about two miles away as the crow flew. The walk helped her to wake up a little more. She loved this time of the morning. There was hardly anyone around, the aroma of dewy grass filled the air and she could hear the dawn chorus as birds welcomed the day.

As she passed a few open windows she heard snoring from inside, and envied those still in their beds, but only briefly. She had the village to herself and she liked it that way.

Whatever was happening in the rest of the world, and whatever was happening in her own life, it gave her a feeling of peace and the sense that maybe the world was not as bad as she thought. This, she knew, was what the servicemen were fighting for. The almost spiritual peace of an English morning. The alternative, it seemed to Betty, was a darkness from which the country and its people would never recover.

She had reached the end of the village when she saw Professor Solomon and Rachel leave their cottage. Like Betty, they were dressed in work clothes. Rachel wore a scarf on her head, but it was black, and with her colouring made her look like a Romany gypsy.

'Good morning, Betty.' The professor tipped his hat.

Rachel smiled in her usual shy way.

'Good morning, Professor. Good morning, Miss Solomon. You're out early today.'

'We made a breakthrough last night, just before it grew dark. We found some pottery, but I've left it in place as I feared breaking it in the dim light. I wanted to get back out as soon as possible today, before anyone else went up there and disturbed anything.'

'How exciting! I'm going that way. Sort of.' It was only slightly off Betty's route to work. 'Would it be OK if I had a look? I shan't bother you for long, as I have to get to the farm on time.'

'Of course, you'll be very welcome. Though I will be showing our finds at the talk on Monday night.'

'I don't think I'm going to be able to make that, Professor. Sorry.'

'Oh, please come.' Betty was surprised to hear Rachel Solomon speak. 'I seldom have a chance to talk to other women at these talks, and you have been so kind to both myself and my father. I would like to know you better. If you do not object.'

'No, not at all,' Betty replied, touched by Rachel's words. 'Very well, I'll come.'

If Mr and Mrs Simpson said anything, Betty could say she had attended because Rachel Solomon asked for her company. It made her feel much easier about the whole thing.

She would like to hear the professor talk. She had grown up in Midchester but knew little about its Roman history. And if she just happened to see Ben whilst she was at the village hall, so be it.

'How long have you lived in Britain?' Betty asked as they walked towards the dig site.

'Ten years now.'

'Where are you from originally?'

It took him so long to answer that Betty was afraid that he had not heard her.

'We are from Poland,' he answered. 'Originally. Our family moved to Germany in the Twenties so I could teach at the university in Berlin. But we left when — when the problems started for our kind.'

'Your kind?' Betty frowned.

'We are Jews.'

'Oh, I see.' Betty nodded to show her understanding. She wanted to ask about the rest of his family, but was afraid of what she might hear.

'There is only myself and Rachel now,' the professor said, as if to answer her question. 'We were lucky. A friend of mine works at Oxford University and he sponsored our escape to Britain. And now he is in the government, so he made sure we do not have to go to an internment camp. I think he has sent me here to keep me out of mischief, but I am not sorry. Midchester is a very interesting little village.'

'It's odd, but I never think of it as being so. Peg is always going on about the intrigue and murders that happen here, but it has always seemed a dull, normal village to me.'

'So you're not excited about the secret Stocking Stealer?' Rachel smiled, which was another surprise for Betty.

'Well, yes, I suppose I am, rather. In fact, I haven't asked you, Rachel. Have you had any stockings stolen?'

Rachel shook her head.

'No, not at all. In fact, I feel a little left out!' She smiled again, and Betty realised that, far from being very serious, Rachel had a good sense of humour. She probably found it hard to smile often, because of the loss of her family, but there was a definite spark of wit in her eyes.

'It is wrong that someone could steal anything in wartime, when everyone else is trying hard to be frugal.'

'Yes, I agree, which is why I think we should find them.'

'Then you are like us,' the professor observed. 'You are digging for facts.'

'With much less success,' Betty said ruefully.

'But your partner, the American. He will help you.'

'He's not my partner!' Betty realised she sounded harsh. 'I mean, he's a friend, that's all.'

'Of course, I would not suggest otherwise,' the professor replied mildly. He and his daughter exchanged amused glances. 'Here we are.'

Betty was relieved to see they had reached the dig site. It looked a bit disappointing to her. She supposed she had expected to see definite parts of the Roman ruins. Apart from one rather precarious flank of wall there was only a big pit, with some stone at the bottom and pots and tools strewn all over the place. One side of the pit had fallen in, which seemed to upset the professor and Rachel.

'It means we will have to start all over again,' the professor explained, after he had spoken rapidly to Rachel in what Betty assumed was Polish. 'The rain last night has caused that side to collapse.'

He pointed to the pile of mud that Betty had noticed.

'Oh, I'm so sorry,' Betty cried. 'I wish I could stay and help, but . . . ' She felt awful leaving them to it, but she also had an existing engagement. She also understood that they might not be in the mood to give her a tour.

'No, no, young Betty. You go and help at the farm. We will manage, do not worry.'

'I'm not working in the morning,' Betty mused. 'Perhaps I could come and help you for an hour or two before the pub opens. I would like to, if I wouldn't be in the way, that is.'

'We will be delighted to have you,' Rachel told her. 'I can show you what to do. What do you say, Papa?'

The professor smiled.

'I think that would be very good. And I promise we will be happier tomorrow.'

'I completely understand why you're upset, professor. If I don't see you later, I'll see you in the morning.'

After arranging a time to meet, Betty waved goodbye and went on to the farm.

When she reached Bedlington Farm, the regular Land Army girls were already hard at work. A few that she knew greeted her before getting on with their work of digging for victory. Betty realised how lucky she was, to be able to work in the pub with her dad most of the time. Some of the girls had told her how miserable their lives were, far away from home. Those who lived in hostels were not so bad, as they had each other for company, but those who lived on the farms were often very lonely and sometimes badly treated by the farmers. Mr Armstrong, who ran Bedlington Farm for the Bedlington family, did look after the girls.

It was for this reason that he liked Betty to take new girls under her wing on their first day. She had more time to take care of them than the conscripted girls, who were too busy to spend time making life easier for newcomers.

* * *

'Ah, there you are, Betty,' Mr Armstrong said when he saw her.

Two girls of about sixteen years of age stood next to him and Betty did not have to be told they were sisters, probably even twins. Both had bright, strawberry-blonde hair and green eyes, with a mass of freckles on their faces and necks. They looked sullen and fretful, but that was not unusual amongst new arrivals. All newcomers were a little nervous when they first joined up.

'I'm sorry I'm late, Mr Armstrong.'

'Only a minute or two, I'm sure.'

'You didn't say that when we were late,' one of the girls interjected.

'You're different, Daisy. Miss Yeardley is not in the Land Army, she comes up to help us voluntarily for two days a week. And very grateful we are for it, too. You have to follow the rules. Of course, if you had not gone off into Shrewsbury last night and missed your last bus home, then you might have been up on time.'

He turned to Betty.

'This is Daisy and her twin sister, Rosie. Will you show them what they need to be doing today?'

'Of course.' Betty did not want to judge too quickly, but she had an idea that Rosie and Daisy were going to be a handful. 'Hello, Rosie. Hello, Daisy.' She smiled to show them that she was a friend, but it did not alter their glum expressions. 'Come with me and I'll show you where to find the tools.'

She took them to a tool shed at the top end of the farm. It was actually more of a barn, with lots of different types of tools, so that there were plenty for each worker. Unfortunately, as metal was in short supply, many of the tools were very old and rusty and didn't always make work much easier.

'You'll find everything you need in here,' she told them. 'Shovels, spades, hoes, hammers, nails — for fixing fences. Shears for the hedges. That's what we'll start you off with today. Hedging.'

'Which is which?' Daisy asked.

'Sorry?' Betty looked puzzled.

'Which is which? Shovels, hoes, shears . . . '

'Don't you know?'

'Nah. We come from London,' Rosie told her. 'We don't know about farming.' Her mouth twisted a little.

Betty took a deep breath.

'OK. This long-handled tool with a flat blade is a spade. That's used for digging. The one with the curved blade is a shovel. It's used for picking things up. The hoe is . . . ' She stopped when she heard the girls start to giggle.

'We're not that stupid!' Daisy was laughing. 'Our dad had an allotment. But you should have seen your face!'

Both girls clung on to each other as if they had made the funniest joke ever.

'Daisy!' Betty felt her face flush red. 'We don't have time for messing around.'

'You've got to have a laugh, haven't you?' Rosie protested, still giggling.

'Grab a pair of shears each and come with me.'

When it was clear they were not going to do so, Betty picked up a pair of shears and thrust them at Rosie. She did the same with Daisy before getting her own pair and leading them out of the shed.

An hour later, she was praying for home time. Rosie and Daisy refused to accept anything she told them. She did not expect them to be perfect at hedge trimming on the first day, but they wouldn't even try.

'Daisy, you could cut a little quicker

and lower than that. One leaf at a time is going to take you for ever.'

'My arms are aching. The shears are too heavy.' Daisy was standing on a box to reach the top of the hedge. Rosie was cutting the side of the hedge, and only doing a slightly better job than her sister.

Betty looked around her to the girls who had been on the land for a while. They all worked so hard, often going home exhausted at the end of the day, too tired to do anything other than crawl into bed and sleep. They had left their homes and families and were often very homesick, but they got on with the job and somehow, despite their exhaustion, managed to remain cheerful. It was just her luck to get these two girls who did not want to do anything at all to help the war effort.

'Have a rest for a few minutes.'

She put down her own shears and stood back to look at the hedge. Where she had cut was a perfectly straight, low line. Where Daisy had cut looked as if it had been barely touched. A whole hour, and it was questionable if she had managed to cut off twenty leaves. The girl would spend several minutes positioning the shears correctly, then even longer trying to snatch at the one leaf she was determined to cut.

'We're rubbish at this!' Rosie sat down on the ground, and brushed some dirt off her new uniform. Betty did not tell her that it would get much dirtier very soon.

'No, of course you're not.' Betty spoke kindly. 'You just need to put in a little more effort, that's all. Watch how I do it.' She went back to the hedge, and deftly trimmed off a chunk of leaves. 'See?'

'I missed it,' Daisy said. 'Show us again.'

'You do it like this — ' Betty stopped, realising that she had been had again, when the girls sniggered.

She turned on them both.

'I'm not afraid of hard work, so I could go on all day if I needed to. But

I'm actually going to sit and watch you do it. Pick up your shears and let's see you make some effort this time.'

'I don't want to.' Rosie slung her shears on the ground next to her.

'Nor me, and you can't make us!' Daisy slumped down next to her sister.

'No, you're right. I can't make you. But I can report you to Mr Armstrong and he can dock your wages for failure to co-operate. He might even send you elsewhere, and believe me, not every farm treats the girls as well as they do at Bedlington Farm!'

'I can't believe anywhere is worse than here,' Rosie grumbled. 'There are no boys, no pictures except in Shrewsbury, nothing to do!'

'There's a pig roast at the back of the pub tomorrow night,' Betty suggested.

'Oh, big deal!' Daisy shot back. 'Lots of old people sitting around eating pork — that's exciting!'

'You do realise there's a war on, don't you? After all, if you're from London, you'll know about the Blitz.'

'Yeah. We lost all our family in it,' Daisy said glumly.

'Oh, I'm sorry.'

'Nah, we didn't.' Rosie giggled. 'We're having you on again.'

'That's no joke, Rosie,' Betty cried, 'considering how many people have lost their lives in the war.'

'Cor, just lighten up, will you?' Daisy snorted. 'You're like an old woman! I mean, do you ever smile?'

Betty sighed and threw down her own shears. It was going to be a very long day indeed.

Fifth Column

'Having a bad day?' A tall, handsome figure stood before Betty. All the other girls were sitting around on hay bales eating their lunch. Rosie and Daisy had wandered off somewhere.

'Ben?' Betty looked up from her slice of bread and jam. 'What brings you here?'

'You do. I went to the pub and your dad told me it was your day on the farm. I'm sorry, I forgot.'

Betty did not know how to reply to that, so she gestured to the space on the hay bale and invited him to sit down.

'Would you like some of my bread and jam?'

'No, you look like you need it more than I do. So,' Ben continued, 'are you having a bad day?'

'I've had better. I've been training

some new land girls and it's taking some doing, I can tell you!'

'I'm sorry I took off yesterday, Betty.'

'I'm sorry if Mr Simpson insulted you.'

'He didn't insult me, he insulted you. How could anyone think that me giving you money was dubious? I thought I'd best leave before I did anything to get me thrown out of your dad's pub. I like Tom, and I don't want to get on his bad side. I like his daughter, too.'

She ignored that.

'I don't think they've thought clearly since Eddie went missing.' She believed she should defend the Simpsons despite their behaviour.

'Maybe, but that doesn't make what they said right.'

'No, it doesn't.'

'So I thought I'd back off a little. I don't want people to talk about you, Betty. But I like being with you, so my resolution to back off didn't last very long.'

'Ooh, I thought you said there were

no boys here!' a voice screeched above them.

Betty looked up to see Rosie and Daisy.

'Girls, this is Captain Ben Greenwood. He's a patient at Bedlington Hall.'

'You look fit enough to me!' Rosie giggled. 'You're the most handsome man I've ever seen.'

'Ben, this is Rosie and Daisy. The new girls.'

'I hope you girls aren't giving Betty here any trouble,' Ben's eyes twinkled. He was clearly amused by the sisters' interest in him.

'It's boring here,' Daisy said by way of an answer. 'Or it was, till you turned up. Do you know where we can go to dance?'

'Not a clue, but we men off fighting the war are relying on you girls to keep the home fires burning and the crops coming in. So you make sure you do what Betty tells you.'

'Yes, Ben,' Rosie said.

'Yes, Ben,' Daisy said.

'I'd better leave you to it.' He stood up.

Betty could tell that his legs were improving. He didn't limp as much, which meant it would not be long before he had to return to the war. The realisation was like a cold hand clutching at her heart.

'Betty, maybe we could go and speak to Mrs Mullins in the morning? Since we didn't manage it yesterday.'

'I'm sorry, Ben, but I promised the professor and Rachel I'd help them on the dig for an hour or two. They've suffered a setback, with a wall caving in. All their pottery has been thrown around.'

'You mean over on that old Roman site?' Rosie butted in.

'Yes.' Betty frowned.

'We thought it was just a load of rubbish,' Daisy said. 'I mean, there's not a real fort there, is there? Just a bit of a wall, and stuff.'

'Then I fell in, which was hilarious!'

Rosie grinned. 'Daisy had to rescue me. The hole caved in.'

'We thought we'd be buried alive!' Daisy laughed.

'You did what?' Betty stood up, aghast. 'Do you realise what you've done? Professor Solomon and his daughter have worked hard up at that site. You've undone all that good work!'

'Well we expected to see a fort and there wasn't one.' Rosie folded her arms. 'It's not our fault if he leaves a hole there for anyone to fall in.'

'I'm going to have a word with Mr Armstrong, and see if he'll let me borrow you in the morning. You can come and clean up the mess you made.'

'We don't have to,' Daisy argued. 'We're here to dig potatoes and the like. Not stupid old ruins that aren't even there.'

'Girls,' Ben said, 'I really think you should do this. In fact, I'll be there, too, and if you don't turn up, I'm going to be really disappointed with you both.'

'Oh,' Rosie said.

'Oh,' Daisy said. 'We'll be there, Ben, we promise. If Mr Armstrong lets us.'

Betty felt her blood boil. Ben had undermined her authority by stepping in and taking over. She did not like it one little bit.

'We'd best get back to work,' she said shortly.

'Betty?' He looked at her quizzically.

'We're very busy,' she said before storming off.

He caught up with her and took her by the arm.

'Betty, what's wrong?'

'You are! They won't do a thing I say, but you step in and they're like putty in your hands.'

'At least they're doing what you want them to do. Isn't that all that matters?'

'They're not doing what I want them to do, Ben. They're doing what *you* want them to do.'

'I'm sorry if I got it wrong. I thought I was helping.'

She breathed in raggedly, and looked

around to see the two girls some way off, whispering to each other.

'You are. I'm sorry. Thank you.' She called to the girls. 'Come on, you two. We have work to do.'

'You're disappointed in me.'

She was, but she could not admit it. She was disappointed that he was vain enough to be swayed by a couple of silly girls, who obviously thought he was the sun and moon all at once.

She had to concede that the girls worked better in the afternoon, relatively speaking. Daisy managed to cut more than a few leaves a time off the top of the hedge, and Rosie did the same with her task. They were still a long way off from working as hard as the other girls, but they did at least seem to be trying, no doubt because they wanted her to give a good report on them to Ben.

They kept stopping every now and then to ask her questions about Ben, such as where did she meet him, and was he her boyfriend. No matter how much she tried to deflect their questions, they came back with more.

'No,' she said, finally. 'Ben is not my boyfriend. My boyfriend, Eddie, went missing in action two years ago. But I'm sure he'll be home soon, and when he does, we're going to get married.'

She had no idea why she told them that. She did not know if Eddie wanted to marry her or not if he returned. She had only said it to stop their questions.

'Is Ben going to be at the pig roast?' Rosie asked.

'Yes, I believe he is coming, and so are some of the servicemen from the airfield and hospital.'

'Then we'll definitely come,' Daisy said.

Mid-afternoon, Mr Armstrong came across to Betty. 'Could you go into Shrewsbury and get some more seed potatoes, Betty? Maybe you could take Daisy and Rosie with you for the run, and so they know where the supplies depot is.' He handed her a set of keys. 'Take the van. I've telephoned the order through, so they're expecting you.'

Daisy and Rosie seemed to like the idea of getting away from the farm a bit, and Betty smiled at their enthusiasm.

'Come on, then, girls. But don't think this means you don't have to work hard! There'll be some lifting to do.'

She was about to leave when she remembered she had not asked Mr Armstrong about the next morning. She hesitated, realising that to do so would get the girls into trouble over damaging the professor's dig. Although they were inclined to giggle and mess around a little, they had worked harder after lunch.

'Mr Armstrong!'

The stricken expressions on the twins' faces decided her.

'What is it, Betty?'

'Since the girls normally only work half a day tomorrow, and I'm not here again till Monday, I wonder if I can borrow them for a while. I'm helping the professor at his dig in the morning, then I could use some extra hands for the pig roast tomorrow night.'

Mr Armstrong thought about it for a moment.

'Yes, I should think that's OK, Betty. I can't really spare the other girls to supervise them tomorrow, and at least it will keep them out of mischief.'

Betty guessed that keeping the two girls out of trouble was going to be high on all their agendas for a while.

'Are you fine with that, Daisy and Rosie?'

'Oh, yes,' they said in unison.

As they walked to where the van was parked, way up at the top of the farm, Daisy took one of Betty's arms, and Rosie took the other.

'Thank you for not getting us in trouble,' Rosie told her.

'Yes, thanks, Betty. You're a pal. Mr Armstrong would have been very angry with us.'

'His bark is worse than his bite, girls. Don't worry. But please promise me to be good in future!'

'We'll do our best, won't we, Daisy?'

'Yeah. We will.'

Betty had doubts about how long that would last, but did not say so. They were behaving well at the moment and she did not want to spoil it by questioning their sincerity. Perhaps all they really needed was someone to believe in them.

'Tell me about your family,' she said instead. 'The truth this time.'

'There's not much to tell,' Daisy said. 'We're from London, and we've got two younger brothers.'

'And three younger sisters,' Rosie added.

'They keep Mum busy.' Daisy said.

'Dad's off fighting the war,' Rosie went on. 'But he owned a garage before then. Our grandad is looking after it whilst Dad is away.'

'Didn't your brothers and sisters get evacuated?'

Betty was coming to realise that talking to one girl was like talking to both of them. They finished each other's sentences, and picked up the conversation where the others left off.

'Mum wouldn't let them go,' Rosie replied.

'She said she didn't want her children going off to strangers,' Daisy explained. 'She cried when we left, but we knew we'd have to do something for the war.'

'We picked the Land Army because we thought it would be nice to be in the countryside.'

'Yet you both hate it here!'

'It's too quiet,' Rosie responded.

'And there's no boys. Except for Ben. He is so dreamy — like a film star!'

'Like Errol Flynn.'

'Or Clark Gable.'

'Except he hasn't got a moustache.' Betty laughed.

'Oh, you know what we mean. He's terribly handsome.'

'Terribly!' Daisy sighed. 'Who's your favourite film star, Betty?'

'I haven't been to the pictures for ages, but I do like Cary Grant.'

'Oh, yes, he's yummy.'

Walking across the field, arm in arm with the twins and talking about film stars, Betty felt like a young girl again. She realised she had been far too harsh with them in the morning. At their age they should have been going out to dances, and learning how to be a woman, not stuck working the fields in the back of beyond.

Not so long ago, she had been just like them, with her head in the clouds over film stars. She remembered giggling a lot, too.

Where had that girl gone to? She seemed to have disappeared as the war began, forced to become a grown up too soon. First by the loss of her mum, and then by the news that Eddie had gone missing. He was not the only young man lost to the village. For many, like Mrs Baker, it was certain their husbands and sons would never return. And wasn't that even more reason to hang on to the joy in life?

* * *

'What are you thinking, Betty?' Daisy asked. 'Are you annoyed with us again?'

They had reached the farm yard where the van was parked.

'Of course not. I was remembering what it was like to be your age, and not worry so much about things.'

'But we want to be older, so we can do what we like,' Rosie told her.

'It doesn't quite work like that, Rosie. The older you get, the more responsibilities you have. You may not think so now, but you're at the best age! Now, come on, those seed potatoes won't carry themselves.'

She moved into the driver's seat, and the girls climbed up on to the bench seat on the passenger side.

Betty put the key in the ignition and turned it. Nothing happened. She tried again. Still nothing happened.

She got out of the car just as Mr Armstrong arrived back at the yard.

'It's not working,' she explained to him.

'Are you sure?'

'I've tried the ignition, but nothing is happening.'

He opened the bonnet and looked inside.

'My goodness,' he said, standing back and running his hands through his hair. 'Someone has taken the rotor arm.'

'What?' Betty felt an icy trickle down her spine. 'When was the last time you used the van, Mr Armstrong?'

'Yesterday. I had to go into Midchester for some groceries. It's been here ever since.'

'Have you seen anyone hanging around?'

Mr Armstrong shook his head.

'No-one.'

Betty hated doing it, but she opened up the passenger door of the car.

'Girls, if you've done this . . . '

'We haven't!' Daisy cried indignantly.

She got out of the van and leaned on the side, closely followed by Rosie who stood in the exact same stance. They folded their arms, and both had tears in their eyes.

'Honestly, Betty, we thought you were our friend now.'

'Anyway,' Rosie pointed out, 'how would we know what a rotor arm was?'

'You said your dad worked in a garage.'

'Yeah, but we don't know anything about cars,' said Daisy. 'We don't listen to anything he says.'

Betty could believe that.

'OK, I'm sorry. It's not the first time something like this has happened lately, and I shouldn't have blamed you. I just thought it might be a prank, that's all.' She turned back to Mr Armstrong. 'It seems as if the person who's been stealing the stockings, and the one who took Peg's rotor arm, has been up here, too.'

'Stealing stockings?' The twins looked surprised.

'We haven't done that!' Rosie pro-tested.

'No, no, I know you haven't. It started before you came here. I shouldn't have blamed you for the rotor arm, either. I knew things were going on, but I hoped there would be a simple explanation.'

'I heard talk that there's a fifth columnist in the area,' Mr Armstrong put in.

'Who told you that?'

'I can't remember now. Someone mentioned it the other day. Or it might have been yesterday, when I was in Midchester.'

'I can understand why a fifth columnist would want to scupper our vehicles, Mr Armstrong,' said Betty. 'But why would he steal stockings and chocolate?'

'It's about morale, Betty, to make everyone fearful. At least, that's the theory I heard. And, now I come to think of it, there was one stranger in the yard earlier today. He wore an American airman's uniform.'

'That was Captain Greenwood,'

Betty explained. 'He came up to see — to see how the work was going on here. He wouldn't do this.'

'Oh, so that was Greenwood, was it? I don't know if you know, Betty, but I've heard his grandfather was German.'

'His great-grandfather, but that doesn't mean he's a spy.'

Mr Armstrong shrugged.

'Well, I suppose blood will out.'

Betty shook her head vehemently.

'No, it won't. Ben is a good man. He would never do a thing like that! I don't know who's been gossiping . . . '

She stopped. There was only one other person who could have known that — Peg Bradbourne. But Peg would not do that to Ben, would she? Betty doubted it, but that did not mean that Peg had not gossiped about Ben's family to someone else. Someone who had taken the information and twisted it. That was the only explanation, surely.

On the other hand, he had been at the farm that afternoon, and Peg had seen him around the village before her stockings went missing. In fact, the thefts had only started after Ben came to Midchester. She only had his word for it that the first time she saw him in the pub had been his first day out. And when Peg's rotor arm went missing, Ben had been alone with the car for a moment or two. Had that been long enough to take out the part? If so, where might he have hidden it?

She checked herself, awash with shame. What on earth was she doing, if not jumping to the same awful conclusions as the gossips? Ben had given her no reason to doubt his honesty. Not to mention the fact that he had almost died fighting in the war.

Mr Armstrong walked away, muttering to himself about having to find another vehicle big enough to carry the seed potatoes.

'Betty,' Daisy said. 'Ben isn't really a spy, is he?'

So already the doubts about him were starting. To make up for her own doubt, Betty would do all she could to nip that rumour in the bud.

'No, of course he isn't. It's ridiculous to even think so. It's just small minds, with nothing better to do than gossip.'

A History Lesson

The talk in the pub that night was all about how there must be a fifth columnist living in Midchester, sabotaging the vehicles.

'First Peg's car, now one of the vans on Bedlington Farm,' Len Simpson commented as he leaned on the bar.

'I hardly see how sabotaging my car is striking a blow against Britain,' Peg called from her usual stool. 'Given the trouble I've had with it over the years, that fifth columnist must have moved in long before we even knew there was going to be a war.'

'It's about morale,' Herbie Potter said.

'And making us distrust each other,' Len added.

'I know I'm no Mata Hari,' Peg said, with a twinkle in her eye. 'More's the pity! I'd have rather liked to be a spy. It gives one a better excuse for watching all the neighbours. As it is, I just have to be a common-or-garden nosey parker!'

'Please try to take this seriously, Peg,' Herbie begged.

'Do you think the stockings were just the start to that?' Betty asked.

'Probably. We all have to be vigilant, and remember, loose lips sink ships.'

'Don't you mean careless talking loses stockings?' Peg quipped.

Herbie and Len tutted and went to their corner.

'Peg?' Betty asked tentatively.

'What, dear?'

'You don't think we have a fifth columnist amongst us, do you?'

'No, of course not. Len and Herbie and the rest of the villagers are determined to be part of this war somehow, and they're just creating a bogeyman to keep them occupied.'

Betty lowered her voice.

'It's got around that Ben's great-grandfather was German, and now Mr Armstrong at the farm suspects him.

Actually, they're saying it was Ben's grandfather now. It won't be long till Chinese whispers turn it into his father.'

'And then Ben himself,' Peg said thoughtfully.

'Exactly.'

'He would hardly be trying to find the Stocking Stealer if it were him, would he?'

'Unless . . . ' Betty's voice trailed off.

'He's using a double bluff?'

'He wouldn't, would he?'

'No,' Peg said emphatically. 'He wouldn't. I'm sorry now that I mentioned it to Mrs Baker when we were talking. I hope you know I didn't mean to implicate Ben in any wrongdoing.'

'No, of course not.'

'It's just that Mrs Baker told me she had some new stockings pushed through her door the other day. She didn't see who left them. When she told me that you and Ben had been to see her, I suggested it might be him, because of the pack he gave me. We got talking, then, about him and his family.'

'Ben left Mrs Baker stockings?'

'I don't know for sure it was him, but I can't think of anyone else who would. Can you?'

'I suppose not.'

She did not know why it bothered her so much. After all, Ben didn't belong to her. It was just that giving stockings to Peg was one thing. She was an elderly woman, and there could be no doubts that he only did it to be kind.

Mrs Baker, on the other hand, wasn't much older than him, and was still quite attractive — when she did not look so tired and run down.

Peg reached across the bar and patted Betty on the arm.

'He's a kind man, Betty. No more, no less.'

'I know that.' She forced a smile and went about her work.

The pub was full, as it always was on a Friday. Every time someone opened the door, Betty could smell fish and chips from the chippy down the road.

Mr Jenson, who owned it, always saved Betty, Tom and Maggie a fish supper each at closing time.

Normally, Betty would long for that moment, especially after a busy day on the farm. As the night went on, the aroma of chips drenched in vinegar would have her mouth watering. Tonight her stomach was churned up with anxiety.

No-one in the pub would have known it. She went about her tasks with her usual smile and cheery manner. But inside her heart felt heavy. Only on her father's insistence did she sit down and eat her supper when the time came. She ate mechanically, feeling each morsel of food hang heavy on her tummy. When she went to bed, she hardly slept due to indigestion. At least, that was what she told herself.

It was three a.m. when she conceded that, despite her best efforts, she was falling for Ben. Why else would she hate the thought of a man she had known for barely a week being a fifth columnist? Why else would she feel so jealous about him leaving stockings for another woman? Why else would it seem that, whenever he was around, the sun shone a little brighter?

More than ever she was determined to find out who the real culprit was and clear Ben's name. Even if she couldn't let him or others know how she felt, she would not have him accused of something he had not done.

At five o'clock, realising that sleep was going to elude her, Betty got out of bed and dressed in her work clothes again, ready to go and help the professor and Rachel.

She sat downstairs, reading the newspaper from the chip wrappings. There was only one subject, as there had been since 1939; the war. The Germans had retreated from Monte Cassino, leaving it to the Allies, albeit at a heavy cost to both sides. A Polish regiment had raised a Polish flag over a monastery to celebrate the moment. It seemed as if the Allies were finally going to take Rome.

It felt symbolic to Betty, with her mother's family being Italian. Perhaps this was the beginning of the end of the war. She said a silent prayer that it would be.

* * *

'You're up early, sweetheart.' Tom came into the kitchen rubbing his eyes.

'I'm helping the professor and Rachel this morning.'

'Don't you have enough to do, what with the pub and the farm? Not that I'm criticising, love. But I worry you do too much.'

'I do a lot of work, Dad, but going to the dig is more like fun. I've never done anything like it before! So it will feel like a rest cure.'

'Your mum had a great interest in history and archaeology. She looked up the history of the pub once.'

'I remember. It was a manor house in Tudor times, wasn't it?'

135

'That's right. It fell into disrepair during the Civil War, so someone turned it into an inn. When it was a manor house the Sheriff of Midchester lived here. He was called Mortimer Something-or-other. They claim he married a witch who was known as the Quiet Woman. Hence the name.'

'There's so much about Midchester I don't know, Dad. I should do what Mum did, and get more involved in local history. I'll have to tell the professor about the Sheriff of Midchester. I think he'd be really interested, unless that's not far back enough for him. Do you want some tea?' She got up from her chair.

'I can do it, sweetheart. Like I said, you do enough.'

She kissed her dad on the head.

'You do a lot, too. Sit down.'

There was a knock on the back door. Betty opened it to see Daisy and Rosie, dressed in their work clothes.

'We thought we'd come and meet you,' Daisy told her.

'In case the professor is angry with us,' Rosie added.

Betty introduced the girls to her dad.

'Ah, so you're the terrible twins, are you?'

'We try not to be,' Daisy said.

'But we just can't help ourselves sometimes,' Rosie said. 'Has Betty said awful things about us?'

'No. She likes you both very much.'

'We like her, too,' Daisy said.

'She's a peach,' Rosie said.

'I hear you're helping us with the pig roast later.'

'Oh, yes.' Daisy nodded. 'We've done that before, so we know what to do.'

'Our street buys and shares a pig, too,' Rosie said. 'It'll be like being home.'

Her eyes filled with tears a little. It struck Betty that they were very young to be away from their mother.

'Do you write to your mum often?'

The girls nodded.

'Oh, yes,' Daisy supplied. 'Every day since we've been here.'

'We've told her all about you and Ben,' Rosie told her.

Tom laughed.

'Our matinee idol. He certainly has all the hearts around here fluttering.'

'He's dreamy,' the girls said together before bursting into giggles.

'Come on,' Betty said, laughing at their enthusiasm for life. 'Let's go and make amends with the professor.'

'Is he very fierce?' Daisy asked.

'No, he's a nice old man,' Betty assured her.

★   ★   ★

The professor took the girl's apology with good grace. Rachel looked less pleased, but she said nothing, probably deferring to her father. They had repaired some of the damage to the pit wall, but it was slow, painstaking work, so he set the girls to work with trowels, teaching them how to move the earth gently. As it did not involve heavy lifting, they took to the work quite willingly.

Betty looked around for Ben, but there was no sign of him.

Things were a little strained at first, but as the girls became engrossed in their work, they started asking the professor questions.

'What are these layers called again?' Daisy gestured to the wall of the pit.

'They are stratifications,' the professor told her. 'Each layer represents hundreds, or even thousands of years in history. But one must be careful. It is easy to be misled.'

'How?' Rosie asked.

'See this wall of stone here?' The professor pointed to a section of the pit which had the remnants of a stone wall going from the top of the pit to the bottom.

'Is that part of the Roman fort?' Rosie asked.

'No, this is the foundation of a house that was built on this spot many years after the Romans came. Probably some time in the Middle Ages. Yet this part here . . . ' he pointed to a layer about six inches up the wall ' . . . is from the Roman era, even though it should be much lower. When men dig foundations for houses, or wells, or anything else that requires digging, including agriculture, it disturbs the stratification. That is why archaeologists have to be very careful with their findings.'

'Tell us about the Romans in Midchester,' Daisy urged.

'Did they throw Christians into pits?' Rosie's eyes shone, which amused Betty. She reminded herself that young girls were often quite bloodthirsty.

'I do not think so.' The professor laughed. 'At least, not here in Midchester. The records, of which there are few, speak of the Midchester prefect being a good man. There is some indication he did not leave when the Romans pulled out of Britain, so his ancestors could well be living in Midchester today.'

'Cor!' Daisy said.

'Do you know who they are?' Rosie asked.

'I am afraid not. Maybe it is Betty.'

Betty laughed.

'My mother was Italian, but her family didn't move to Britain till the turn of the century. As far as I know, we don't have centurions in the family.'

'But, Betty,' the professor said, 'the Roman who stayed here might have married an Anglo-Saxon girl. Or their children could have. It could be on your father's side.'

'Now I'm going to have to find out!' Betty decided.

Whilst they worked, the professor enthralled them all with the history of the Roman invasion of Britain. He was an enthusiastic tutor, and he had an equally enthusiastic audience in Betty, Daisy and Rosie.

Soon it was time to go. The girls groaned.

'Can we come back another time, Professor?' Rosie asked. 'We've really enjoyed helping, and you're much better at talking about history than our teachers.'

Professor Solomon nodded.

'You will be welcome, girls. You have worked well this morning.'

'Can women become archaeologists?' Daisy asked.

'Of course. My daughter, Rachel, has a doctorate in archaeology, do you not, Rachel?'

'I don't know if we're clever enough for that,' Rosie demurred.

'Perhaps you could work on some digs,'

Rachel suggested, having warmed to the girls over the course of the morning. It was hard not to. Even though they could be silly at times, there was no real harm in them.

'We know many archaeologists who work their way up, then present their papers later.'

'If Mum and Dad let us,' Daisy warned. 'I think they'd rather we worked in a shop or a hairdresser's.'

'Yeah. We'll just have to tell them that we want to be archaeologists, Daisy.'

'We'd best be going,' Betty put in.

'Professor, Rachel, are you coming to the pig roast tonight?'

'We must respectfully decline,' the professor told her.

Betty put her hands to her mouth.

'Oh, I'm so sorry! That was thoughtless of me. You don't eat pork, do you?'

'But the invitation was welcome, Betty,' Rachel said with her sad smile. 'Perhaps I can persuade Papa to come along later for a drink.'

'Yes.' The professor beamed. 'I think that would be acceptable.'

The three girls walked back towards Midchester arm in arm.

'I like the professor,' Daisy said.

'Rachel is nice, too,' Rosie said. 'Though I don't think she liked us to begin with.'

'She's always very quiet,' Betty explained. 'They've known a lot of sadness in their lives.'

The girls huddled in closer. It made Betty feel like a protective big sister. In many ways that was what she was becoming to these two giggly girls.

Betty began to think about Ben, and why he had not turned up for the dig as he promised he would. She wondered if it was because she had been so short with him the day before. She regretted her behaviour now, especially since she had built up such a good rapport with the sisters. She had been silly to consider he had undermined her, when all he had done was try to help her with them.

* * *

She was glad to see that the girls worked well for the rest of the day, helping to set up the pig roast. They happily baked bread with Betty and the other women, and didn't mind sweeping up when needed. They did have the tendency to break out into giggles at the silliest things, but their laughter was refreshing and made Betty, Tom and Maggie smile.

They even helped with clearing tables and washing glasses during the lunch time trade, although they were not allowed to serve drinks due to their age.

'What a pair of poppets,' Peg said when she arrived to sit on her usual stool and after Betty had introduced them.

'Yes, they are,' Betty agreed. 'I think Dad would adopt them, if he could. I thought they were going to be trouble when I first met them yesterday, but I suspect they just like to know why they're doing something, instead of just being told to do it. They were as good as gold on the dig this morning.'

'Did you know, Miss Bradbourne,' Daisy interrupted, 'that there were Romans in Midchester nearly two thousand years ago?'

'I had heard.'

'They left us to it, though,' Rosie chipped in. 'Because of all the fighting in Rome about who was going to be emperor.'

Daisy took up the story.

'Then the Normans and the what-nots came and took over.'

'I don't think I'm familiar with the whatnot tribe.' Peg winked at Betty.

That tickled the twins and they laughed about it for the rest of the afternoon.

'I wish we could do this all the time,' Daisy said, putting some glasses on the bar. 'Archaeology in the morning, then the pub in the afternoon.'

Rosie nodded enthusiastically as she took the glasses from her sister and set them in the sink to wash.

'It's much more interesting than digging potatoes.'

'But we rely on the land girls to feed us all,' Tom pointed out. 'Otherwise we'd starve, because we can't buy food in from abroad any more.'

'We never thought of it like that,' Rosie said. 'We'll try and work harder on Monday, Tom.'

Betty laughed. She wished that she had been as quick at wrapping the girls around her little finger as her dad and Ben were.

'How is it that you know just what to

say to them?' she asked him, when they had a minute.

Tom raised an eyebrow and smiled.

'You were sixteen once.'

She grinned, remembering how sullen she used to get when asked to do anything at that age.

'Yes, but they're double the trouble!'

Tom winked.

'You reckon?' he said.

'He's Not Coming Home!'

When the pub closed for the afternoon, everyone started on the real preparations for the pig roast. The garden at the back of the pub was as big as the village green, so all the stalls were set up along the path. Some of the women had saved their ration coupons so they could get enough flour to bake cakes and other tasty treats.

Other stalls sold bric-à-brac, and there was tombola with small prizes of stockings, chocolate, bottles of beer and other luxuries that were hard to come by during the war. The money raised, over and above the cost of another pig, would be used to help those who had lost loved ones in the fighting.

Mrs Baker turned up with her five children in tow, and immediately set about working. The children ran around happily whilst their mother worked, apart from the youngest, who was five. He was a quiet child who stayed next to his mum at all times.

'Little Michael doesn't talk much,' Mrs Baker explained to Betty. 'He doesn't mix very well. But he's a good boy.'

'I can see that,' Betty said. 'But if you need any help with him, just ask. If I can't help, I'm sure Rosie and Daisy will. They have younger brothers.'

The twins had already elected themselves carers of Mrs Baker's other children. The eldest boy, who was a couple of years younger than they were, clearly thought they were wonderful. His serious young eyes spoke of true devotion. Rosie and Daisy took his adoration in their stride, whilst loving every minute of it.

The men had put down a temporary dance floor, and a group of young men from the airfield who had formed a Glenn-Miller-style jazz band were coming along to play.

Pride of place, however, was the pig,

roasting over a spit in the centre of the garden.

Ben, Charlie and Fiona arrived late in the afternoon, and immediately set about helping. It gave Betty little chance to talk to Ben, other than to say hello. She did notice that he looked paler than usual.

'Is Ben OK?' she asked Fiona when she had a chance.

'He's been overdoing it, determined to get better and get back in action,' Fiona said. 'He walked too far yesterday again. He wanted to go out this morning but the doctor overruled him. He was only allowed out this afternoon because we have Peg's car.'

Whilst Betty was sorry Ben was feeling unwell, she was glad to know the reason he had not turned up for the dig.

Tom set about putting everyone where they needed to be.

'Betty, Maggie, you tend the outside bar. I'll be inside, although I doubt there'll be many in there tonight. Daisy,

Rosie, will you take care of the soft drinks? Give the younger children squash and the older children pop.'

'What can we do?' Ben asked.

'I think you need to rest, young man, from what I've heard.'

'Come on. There must be something even an old crock like me can do.' There was bitterness in Ben's voice that Betty had not heard before.

'How about you and Charlie blow up some balloons for the children?' Tom suggested. 'You can sit down to do that.'

'Sure.' Ben's glum expression told Betty that he was not happy.

'Can I get you a drink?' she asked shyly. 'It can only be lemonade or something until opening time, but it's a hot day.'

He smiled and it seemed as if the sun shone a little brighter again.

'Thanks, Betty. And maybe you can come and talk to me for a few minutes, if you're not too busy. We've still got a mystery to solve.'

'Funny you should say that. Mrs Mullins has just come in with Peg. We could have a chat with her. I'll get Peg to bring her over.'

Before speaking to Peg, Betty fetched drinks for Ben, Charlie and Fiona.

'Can we be detectives too?' Daisy asked when Betty asked for the soft drinks. 'We could talk to everyone and ask what their alibis are, like in the films.'

'Go on, then.' Betty felt it could do no real harm. 'Just stick to the children, though.'

'Can we frisk them?'

'Certainly not!'

Betty laughed so much she almost spilled the drinks. As she walked back to Ben, she could not remember when she had enjoyed herself as much as she had today. At least not since the war began.

'What are those two up to now?' Ben asked.

Charlie and Fiona were seated opposite him, doing their best to blow up some very stubborn balloons.

'They want to frisk the children.'

Ben laughed.

'Shall we do that to everyone who arrives tonight? If we find a pair of stockings and a rotor arm in their pockets we're home free!'

'No!' Betty put the drinks down and sat down. 'I'm sorry to hear your legs are bad. We missed you at the dig today. Ben, I was afraid I'd offended you yesterday. If I did, I'm sorry. I know you were only trying to help with the girls.'

'You were right to be annoyed. It seems to me that you and Tom are doing a good job with them.'

'They're too young to be so far away from their mum,' she said. 'I think that's the only reason they get a bit wild sometimes. They've been as good as gold today.' Betty looked at her watch. 'Time is getting on. I'll go and fetch Peg and Mrs Mullins before it starts to get busy.'

Betty and Peg helped Mrs Mullins across the garden, where Ben stood up and held out a chair for her.

'Oh, such nice manners,' she twittered. 'All the American airmen have, I find.'

'Do you get many at your cottage?' Peg quizzed mischievously.

'You know what I mean, Peg Bradbourne. Well, isn't this exciting, having a fifth columnist amongst us? I hear he's American . . . '

'Mrs Mullins,' Betty broke in, 'we wanted to ask you if you saw anything the other day, when Peg's car was sabotaged. Your cottage looks right over that street.'

'I don't spend all day at the window, dear.'

Peg coughed and gave Betty a meaningful look.

'I'm sure you don't.'

'What time was it?'

'It would have been between around ten and eleven,' Fiona offered. 'Charlie and I had been walking around talking to people. Not that we got much information. It was pretty much the same. They got up, did their chores, then they either went out to work or opened their post.'

'That's what I was doing at that time,' Mrs Mullins said. 'I'd had a letter from my sister, Petunia. She lives up in Glasgow, and she always writes such long, lovely letters, all about her daughter and grandchildren. Her daughter works for the government on something to do with the war, but she's not allowed to say what. Her son-in-law is in one of those prisoner of war camps, and we all club together to send him Red Cross parcels. Petunia said that . . . '

'So you didn't see anything?' Peg cut her short.

'Not really. Except this young man.' She pointed to Ben.

'That was later,' Betty pressed. 'When we returned and Ben found the rotor arm missing.'

'Yes, that might have been it.'

Betty was not happy about the 'might', but it seemed to be the best Mrs Mullins could do. Every story was the same. People were going about their daily business, then either stockings or chocolate went missing or vehicles were sabotaged.

'What was that about an American fifth columnist?' Ben asked.

'Oh, yes,' Mrs Mullins replied. 'They say his father was German. Or it might have been his grandfather.'

'Actually, it was my great-grandfather.' Ben spoke through tight lips. 'Is this what people are saying about me, Betty?'

'I . . .'

'What Betty wants to say,' Peg said, 'is that it's plainly nonsense and that no-one with any common sense is giving the rumour credence.'

'Yes, that's exactly what I wanted to say.'

'Thank you both.'

Ben went very quiet after that.

As the garden began to fill up with early arrivals, she had to go and start serving on the outside bar.

'I'll see you later, Ben,' she said. 'Perhaps you could save me a dance. If you want to, that is.'

Even though it was forward of her to ask, it would help if it was seen that Betty did not distrust Ben.

'That's the best offer I've had since the war began.'

It seemed to do everyone good to forget about the war for a few hours. Children ran around the lawn, pretending to be aeroplanes or soldiers fighting Hitler, but even that did not dampen the atmosphere. All the women were in their best summer frocks, and the men in their Sunday suits. Betty wore a dress of yellow, dotted with blue forget-menots. It had been her mother's, bought in the nineteen-thirties, but Betty had managed to modernise it a little.

The twins wore matching white broderie anglaise dresses, emphasising their youth. They were both good with the children, keeping the smaller ones out of mischief like two protective aunties. It was hard for Betty to equate them with the sulky girls she had met only the day before.

The aroma of pork filled the air, making everyone's mouth water. After all the hardships and sacrifices, it was good to smell decent food again. They might not all get more than one good slice each, but that did not matter, and neither did it stop the party atmosphere. Good friends and good food went a long way to making one forget about the troubles in the world.

The band arrived and started playing Glenn Miller tunes, along with some classics the older people in the audience enjoyed. Everyone joined in with 'Apple Blossom Time', which for a short time reminded them of their loved ones far away.

Mrs Baker, who had helped out on the stalls, danced with Herbie Potter. Betty noticed she was wearing her new stockings, and she felt a pang thinking about it. Yet Ben showed no signs of interest in Mrs Baker, as far as Betty could tell.

When Daisy and Rosie had finished

dispensing soft drinks to the children, they stood at the side of the stage, watching the handsome young musicians and giggling to each other. From her vantage point at the bar, Betty exchanged glances with her father, who had just popped outside. He nodded, as if to tell her it was harmless enough fun for a couple of teenage girls.

Suddenly the band struck up 'In The Mood' and Betty felt someone reach for her hand across the bar.

Ben smiled at her.

'You promised me a dance.'

'To this?' She laughed, but was a little worried. 'Are you sure you should?'

'Hey, I'm not that much of an old crock!'

'I don't know if I should yet.' She looked at the queue of customers.

'Go on!' Maggie was helping to serve at the outside bar. 'Go and dance whilst you still can.'

Betty joined Ben on the dance floor, where they started to jitterbug, cheered on by those watching. He seemed to forget his bad leg as he spun her around. The music swept her away, making her feel like the girl she was, rather than the aged woman who had practically worn widow's weeds since Eddie went missing. If the Simpsons disapproved, she did not care at that moment.

The song ended, but the band struck up with another, slower number. Betty was about to walk away, before she realised that Ben still had hold of her hand.

'You're not escaping that easily.' He pulled her into his arms.

The slow dance was more intimate than the fast dance, which did nothing to calm Betty's nerves. She told herself that she only stayed out of good manners. It had nothing to do with how nice it was to be close to him.

'You're only doing this because you've overdone it and need someone to lean on,' she teased, trying to take the emotion out of the situation.

'Can I lean on you when I need it,

Betty?' he asked in a gentle voice.

'Of course. We're friends, aren't we?'

'Sure.' The tone in his voice suggested that it was not the answer he wanted.

'You really should be careful,' she said, to keep the conversation away from all the things they wanted to say to each other but which they could not. 'Don't overdo it.'

'Don't overdo what? The walking? Or the wanting to be with you?'

She looked up into his clear blue eyes.

'I never know when to take you seriously.'

'I'm serious now.'

'Ben, you know how difficult things are for me. With the Simpsons and everything.'

'I know.' Ben sighed. 'Betty, I don't want to push you into anything, but in the short time we've had together, I've really come to like you. Can I hope you like me a little?'

'You can hope,' she said mischievously. Then, realising he was being

161

serious for a change, she whispered against his ear, 'I do like you.'

Because the dance was slower, she had time to look around her. She could see Mr and Mrs Simpson standing at the edge of the dance floor, whispering to each other and some of their friends. She instinctively knew that they were talking about her, and she moved away from Ben a little.

'Did I say something wrong?'

'No. I just . . . everyone's watching.'

'Not everyone.'

'The Simpsons are.'

'I thought you liked me.'

'I do.'

'But clearly not enough to throw caution to the wind.' Ben pulled away and gave her a brief, mocking bow. 'Thank you for the dance, Miss Yeardley. I won't bother you for another one.'

'Ben . . . '

He walked away from her and back towards his seat.

Feeling adrift without a dance partner, Betty looked around her. Daisy and

Rosie were talking to two of the musicians, who were taking a break during the slower dances. Both were looking up at the men with admiration. One of the men whispered something to Daisy, who transmitted the message to Rosie. Rosie stood back a little and shook her head. She began arguing with her sister.

The young man who had been talking to Rosie walked away in a huff, but the other took Daisy's hand, and Betty saw him mouth, 'Let's get out of here.'

She looked around for her father, or someone else who could help. The man, although only in his late twenties, was still a lot older than Daisy. She walked over and put her hand on Daisy's arm.

'Where are you going?' she asked lightly. 'You're supposed to be helping us to clear up.'

'We're just going for a walk,' Daisy said, giggling. She seemed to have no real idea of the man's intentions.

'I told her not to go.' Rosie scowled.

'Shut up, Rose. It's just a bit of fun, that's all. Come on, Harry.' Daisy put her arm in his, trying to act grown up, but looking even more like the child she was.

'Daisy, I don't think this is a good idea,' Betty pleaded.

'And you should know better, Harry,' a voice said from behind her.

Betty breathed a sigh of relief. She would not know how to deal with the American musician, but Ben would.

'Leave her alone. She's just a kid.'

'I'm sixteen,' Daisy said indignantly, whilst trying to pull herself up to her full height.

'In America that's jailbait,' Ben said. 'And Harry knows it.'

The two men eyed each other for a moment or two. Ben was taller than Harry, but Harry didn't have a bad leg to hold him back. Still, Ben had a more forceful personality.

'She's too young for you.'

Harry let go of Daisy's arm.

'Never mind, kid,' he smirked. 'It was

nice while it lasted.' He walked back towards the podium and picked up his instrument.

'You've ruined my life!' Daisy exclaimed, with the drama of which only sixteen-year-old girls were capable.

'Nope,' Ben drawled. 'Just your evening. Not even the whole evening. You've been having a good time up to now. Believe me, honey, if the worst thing that happens to you in your life is being rescued from a guy with no morals, you're going to have it pretty good.'

Daisy flounced off with her sister in tow. But Betty could not help noticing that Rosie looked relieved. She had been genuinely worried about her sister's welfare, and it was good to know that Daisy had her sister looking out for her. Clearly Rosie's head was screwed on a little tighter.

'Thanks for helping, Ben,' Betty said shyly.

'You're welcome. It's guys like that who give the rest of us a bad name.'

'I'd best be getting back to help Maggie at the bar.' She started to walk away.

'Betty?'

'Yes?'

'I'm sorry about earlier. I didn't act in a very gentlemanly way after the dance, leaving you there like that.' He grimaced. 'I guess it's also guys like me who give us a bad name!'

'I've never seen you behave in any way less than perfect, Ben. You're kind, too, giving stockings to Peg and Mrs Baker . . .'

'Whoa, hold on there a minute. Mrs Baker? I didn't give her stockings. Did she say that I did?'

'No, she said someone pushed them through her letterbox. I just thought that, as you'd given Peg some, you'd done the same for Mrs Baker, after hearing her story about not affording a new pair.'

'It wasn't me, Betty. I don't think it would be proper, her being a young widow with children and all that. She

might get the wrong idea … '
Realisation dawned on his face. 'Oh, I
get it. You thought I was sweet on her!
That's why you're not sure about me.'

'No. I mean, I didn't know what to
think, except for thinking that you'd
been kind and all that.' Betty became
flustered and red in the face.

'I'm not like Harry, I promise.'

She put her hand on his arm.

'I know you're not, Ben.'

He stroked her cheek, and for a
moment their eyes locked. His face
drew nearer to hers and all around her
the noise seemed to disappear. This was
reality now; her and Ben, alone
together. She knew that, if he kissed
her, her fate would be sealed, and she
longed to be kissed …

'You're a fine one!' Daisy said from
beside her. It was a surprise to Betty to
see that she was actually standing next
to them. The Simpsons were also close
by, watching everything. 'Telling me
how to live my life, when you're kissing
the captain. I wonder what your Eddie

will say when he comes back and thinks you're going to marry him.'

'I hardly think that's any of your business,' said Ben. 'Besides, who told you Betty was going to marry him?'

'I did,' Betty said in a small voice.

She looked around for a handy hole to jump into, but there were none around.

'When?' Ben frowned.

'Yesterday,' Daisy said, 'when we were cutting the hedges. She said that you're not her boyfriend and that she's going to marry Eddie when he returns. Isn't that right, Rosie?' She turned to her sister who had joined them.

'Yes. But . . . ' Rosie looked uncomfortable, as if she understood the situation better than Daisy ' . . . it's not our business, Daisy.'

Ben was looking at Betty with intensity.

'I guess I've been misled,' he said quietly.

'Ben, I never misled you,' Betty cried. 'You've known all along that I'm waiting for Eddie to return.'

'You didn't tell me you planned to marry him.'

Betty couldn't reply. With the Simpsons listening in, looking very smug, she could hardly admit that she had told the twins that just to stop them asking questions.

'It's as it should be,' Len Simpson called over. 'We don't need you Yanks coming over here, making our young women forget their promises.'

'Believe me, sir,' Ben said through clenched teeth. 'I know better than anyone the effects of a broken promise. But I also know the danger of false hope.'

Betty put her hand to her mouth. She could see the pain in Mrs Simpson's eyes.

'You may not want to hear it,' Ben said, carrying on, 'but I am going to say it. Eddie is not coming home. The sooner you realise that, the sooner you can all move on.'

'Ben, that's a dreadful thing to say!'

'No, Betty, it's an honest thing to say. I know you're all tucked away from the war here, so you don't think it can touch you, but I've been out there, in the thick of things. I know what 'missing in action' means.'

Mrs Simpson started to weep quietly.

'Even if I did like you, Ben Greenwood, what you've just done has finished it, as far as I'm concerned!' Betty went to put her arms around Mrs Simpson's shoulders. 'That was cruel and unnecessary.'

He brushed his hands through his hair.

'Mrs Simpson, I'm sorry to have hurt you, ma'am. I don't want to cause anyone pain.'

'Then you'd best be going,' Len Simpson growled. 'Before you cause any more trouble.'

'Yeah, I'll get out of your way.'

Ben may have been replying to Mr Simpson, but he was looking at Betty as he said it.

'I won't stay where I'm not wanted.'

As he walked away, Betty wanted to run after him, to explain. But she was also angry with him. She knew that he had said what everyone else had been avoiding for the past two years.

But she could not bear to see Mrs Simpson cry.

Betty hadn't thought the evening could get worse, but it did. At around nine-thirty, the professor and Rachel arrived. Betty, her father and Maggie welcomed them, making sure they had a table with drinks and food, but everyone in the vicinity became quiet. There were whispers of 'fifth columnist' amongst the crowd.

'I think we have outstayed our welcome,' the professor said, putting down his drink only five minutes after arriving.

'No,' Betty said. 'You haven't. You're very welcome. Aren't they, Dad?'

'Absolutely,' Tom assured them. 'Betty has been telling us all about your dig. I'd love to hear more about it.'

The professor started to tell Tom

what he had told Betty and the twins, but the atmosphere at the party had changed. A few people danced, but most sat silently, watching the professor with suspicion.

'It is time we left. Goodnight.' He stood up.

'Goodnight,' Rachel said, taking her father's arm.

Betty did not know if she imagined it, but the professor seemed a little shorter when he left than when he'd arrived. She looked around her, angrily, wanting to tell everyone what a disgrace they were.

'Time to clear up, sweetheart,' Tom said. 'If anyone wants anything else they can order it inside.'

'Dad . . . '

'I know, but there's nothing to be done about it at this moment, love. We'll sort it out. I promise.'

War Fatigue

Several weeks passed. Betty saw Ben occasionally in the village, when he went to the post office, but they did not speak much. She busied herself in the pub and on the farm. Daisy seemed to have got over her fit of pique, and though quieter than usual, she greeted Betty warmly enough. On Saturday mornings they fell into the way of helping the professor on the dig.

One Sunday morning, Betty went to church with her father and Maggie, then meandered home, half hoping to bump into Ben so she could explain to him about Eddie. She realised that she was partly to blame for his anger and what he had said.

It might seem that she had led him on by telling him she liked him, just before he heard that she apparently intended to marry Eddie all along.

Lunchtime in the pub was quiet. Rosie came on her own and sat outside drinking lemonade. It was strange to see her without her sister.

'Daisy isn't speaking to me, or anyone, at the moment,' she explained. Betty had gone outside to sit next to her on the bench for a few minutes. 'I know she's sorry for what she said about you and Eddie, and she's OK while we're working, but something's not right with her.'

'Daisy only told the truth. I did tell you both that I intended to marry Eddie. When you see her, tell her that I'm sorry if I upset her.'

'She'll get over it. Daisy's always falling in love with someone or other. I can't be bothered. Not that I don't like boys, but they all seem a bit stupid sometimes. Now, if I could find someone like Ben, I'd be happy.' Rosie blushed. 'Sorry. I know he's too old for me. But he is kind, really. I mean, I know what he said about Eddie wasn't nice, but I think it was the truth. You know?'

'Yes,' Betty admitted. 'But the Simpsons aren't ready to accept that yet, and it was cruel of him, as an outsider, to say it. Anyway, I'm not with Ben, so you don't have to apologise to me for liking him.'

'You do like him, though. I know you only said that about Eddie because we were asking so many questions.'

'You're a smart girl.'

'Daisy is, too,' Rosie said, defending her sister. 'She's the clever one, except when it comes to boys. Mum was strict with us, you see, so now we're away from home, Daisy has gone a bit mad.'

'She'll learn.' Probably the hard way, Betty thought sadly, though she did not say that to Rosie.

'I wish Mum were here.' Rosie had tears in her eyes.

Betty put her arm around her and gave her a hug.

'Come on, love. Nothing is that bad. So Daisy made a bit of a fool of herself over a fella! We all do it, at least once.

It's part of being alive, and one day none of this will seem important.'

Betty did not miss the irony of her saying that to Rosie, when she herself was so worried about public opinion.

'I'm not your mum, but I can be your big sister whilst you're here. You can probably tell me things you daren't tell your mum.'

Rosie smiled through her tears.

'You're a good pal, Betty. Do you think this war will ever be over so we can go back to how we were?'

'I hope so, darling. I really do. Though I don't know if things can ever be exactly as they were.' Betty turned to see her dad standing on the doorstep of the pub. 'Sorry, Dad, I'm coming now.'

'No rush, sweetheart.' He walked across and gave Rosie a friendly pat on the shoulder. 'Don't you worry, little one. Our Betty will look out for you, and so will I.'

The Simpsons came in for a drink near to closing time.

'What can I get you?' she asked

brightly, determined not to air any more dirty linen in public.

'Half a pint for me and lemonade for Myrtle,' Len said.

Myrtle Simpson had gone into the ladies' lounge to join her friends. She kept putting her hankie to her eyes, which suggested she was telling the other ladies about the party. When Betty took Myrtle her drink, she was thanked coolly. The murmuring began as she moved away again.

'He had the nerve to come down and see Len this morning to say he was sorry,' Myrtle said in a stage whisper. 'Len sent him away with a flea in his ear.'

Peg sat at her normal seat on the bar, listening thoughtfully.

'Ben Greenwood is right, you know,' she suddenly said, half turning in her seat. 'And you all know he's right. You've all gone on about how you wish Myrtle would face the fact Eddie is dead. It's just that you haven't had the courage to say it to her face.'

'Well, I never,' one of the ladies said. 'I'm sure we've said nothing of the sort.'

'Yes, you have said it. Myrtle, dear, no-one wants to cause you any pain, but it seems to me that you're prolonging your own pain. Not just yours, either.' Peg glanced towards Betty. 'I don't blame you for hoping, but is it hope, or do you think you deserve more sympathy, say, than Mrs Baker? Keeping Eddie alive does that for you.'

'You're a cruel woman, Peg Brad-bourne!'

'I dare say, but it's also cruel to come between a young couple because of your own false hopes.'

'My Eddie is alive. I know it! I feel it!'

'I hope you're right.' Peg finished her stout.

'I know my own son better than a man who is probably a Nazi sympa-thiser! He's in league with that professor. I saw him coming out of the professor's house before he came to us — talking like they were old friends, they were. I'll warrant they're the ones who have been stealing stockings and messing with vehicles.'

'What proof do you have of this?' Betty cried.

'Proof? That Ben has a German grandfather . . . '

'Great-grandfather!'

' . . . and the professor is from Germany.'

'He's from Poland originally,' Betty argued. 'He moved to Germany to work, but left when his people were persecuted. He lost all his family.'

'So he tells us.'

'Has he given you any reason not to believe him?'

'His digging could be an excuse to find out things about us.'

'To find out the Romans were here thousands of years ago!' Betty laughed. 'I hardly think that's a State secret.'

'We need to speak to him.' Herbie Potter had arrived. 'We have to flush out these fifth columnists where we can.'

'He's an elderly man,' Betty protested. 'And he's known a lot of sadness in his life. Leave him alone!'

'It seems to me, Betty Yeardley,' Myrtle said, 'that you care a bit too much about outsiders and not enough about the people you were brought up with. You just wait till my Eddie gets back and I tell him what you've been up to. He'll not want to marry you then.'

Betty resisted the urge to cheer.

'I think you're wrong, and I think we should avoid pointing the finger at people just because of their ancestors or where they've lived. What are we fighting the war for, if not to stop that sort of persecution?'

'Closing time!' Tom rang the bell.

'Couple of minutes yet!' Herbie looked at the clock.

'It's closing time when I say it's closing time,' Tom said firmly. 'I've had enough. You're not plotting against innocent people in my pub!'

'And what were Betty and her friends doing in the snug last week, if not plotting?' Len Simpson said.

'We weren't pointing the finger at anyone in particular. We were just trying to find out who'd done it before we started accusing innocent people.'

'Dad, what's happening?' They were upstairs and had invited Maggie, Peg and Rosie for lunch. It was mostly the leftovers from the day before. 'The professor has been here for years. He's almost as much a part of this village as the Simpsons or Herbie.'

'I don't know what's up with our Herbie,' Maggie put in. 'He's been funny ever since his girlfriend, Floss, went to stay with her sister in Wales.'

'I feel sorry for the Simpsons.' Peg bit into a sandwich, 'but I don't see why Myrtle thinks she's more deserving of sympathy than anyone else in this war. She's not the only one to lose a loved one. And now they're taking out their grief on others. As you said, Betty, if we persecute others, just like Hitler, what are we fighting for in the first place?'

'The professor is nice.' Rosie was happy to be included. 'I don't believe he or Rachel would spy on anyone.'

'I don't know what this village is coming to.' Peg said.

'It's war fatigue. I saw it in the last war.' Tom's face took on a haunted look that Betty recognised. 'At first, everyone is almost excited to be at war, and we all pull together. But as time goes on and there seems to be no resolution, people not caught up in the thick of the fighting start to distrust each other. It's sad, but part of human nature. Len and Myrtle are good people, but losing their son in such an uncertain way is bound to affect them.'

'Yes.' Maggie nodded. 'At least I could bury my husband. They can't mourn Eddie. So they keep the hope of him being alive as a monument to him.'

'Perhaps I was cruel.' Peg sighed.

Maggie patted her arm.

'It's something they've needed to hear for a long time.'

'Besides,' Tom said, 'Myrtle is quick enough to speak her mind. If she can't take it, she shouldn't hand it out.'

There was a loud knock on the downstairs door. Betty went to answer it and found Ben standing outside.

'I need to talk to you.' His normal humour seemed to have deserted him, and he looked dark under his eyes.

'I heard that you went to apologise to the Simpsons. That was good of you.'

'It didn't help, I'm afraid. Will you come for a walk with me, Betty? Maybe we could take the path to Bedlington Hall? I'd really like to speak to you alone.'

Betty nodded and shouted up to her father that she was going out.

'Hang on, Betty, I'll come with you!' Rosie shouted. 'It's time I was getting back to the farm. Daisy will wonder where I am.'

Rosie left them at the turn off to Bedlington Farm. They waved to her and carried on up towards the hall.

'Betty, I . . . '

'Ben, I . . . '

They laughed awkwardly.

'You first.'

'No, ladies first.'

'I wanted to explain about what I said to Daisy and Rosie. They were asking me all sorts of awkward questions so I just blurted out the first thing that came into my head.'

'Are you sure it wasn't the first thing you thought of because it's what you want?'

'No. I mean, of course I want Eddie to be alive, but you and Peg were right. He's not coming back.'

'Peg?'

Betty quickly explained what had happened in the pub. She faltered a little over the accusations of Ben and the professor being fifth columnists, but she felt he deserved the truth about what people were saying.

'I called on the professor to apologise for not turning up to the dig as I'd promised, that was all. I can't believe what people are saying. He's done nothing to deserve it.'

'Dad says it's war fatigue.'

'Yeah, I guess you're right. Betty, I wanted to apologise for the night of the pig roast. I know I probably made things worse for you, but I feel as if we're going around in circles. And now . . . '

'Now what?'

'I've applied to return to the war.'

'Ben, you're not well enough!'

'I reckon I can cope with a bit of a limp. It won't be tomorrow. It'll be in a couple of weeks or so. Anyway, I wanted you to know.'

'Oh.'

'I'm going to miss this little village and I'm going to miss you, but I won't ask you to wait for me, Betty. That wouldn't be fair.'

She wanted to beg him not to go.

'I wish you would think about it a bit more.'

'When the locals turn against you, it's time to get out.'

'I haven't turned against you, Ben.'

'Thank you for that. But as special as this time has been for me, it's time to get back. I want to be there when we take Berlin. I just wanted to ask you something.'

'What's that?'

'Fiona and Charlie are talking about taking in a movie tomorrow night. Will you come? No strings, nothing that's going to get you into trouble. Just come along as our friend. It'll be the last chance for us all to get together, I guess.'

'Yes, Ben, I'll come.'

A Night Drive

It was a subdued group of friends who went into Shropshire to the pictures on the Monday night. It was obvious that Fiona and Charlie had become very close, but their life together was uncertain.

'I don't know if I'm going to get a transfer,' Fiona explained to them on the way there. 'But I'm going to do my best. Charlie needs me.'

As for Ben, Betty felt they were in some sort of limbo. Their relationship could not move on, and yet they could not go back, either.

The film was a double feature. It started with a Three Stooges comedy, with an extended scene about baseball which Charlie and Ben found hilarious. The second feature, 'The Man In Grey', was more to the girls' liking, but a bit too melodramatic for the boys.

'James Mason is so delicious,' Fiona whispered across to Betty. 'Even as the baddie!'

Afterwards the four got a bag of chips each and walked through Shrewsbury, eating them and talking about anything but the impending departure of Ben and Charlie. They managed to catch the last train back to Midchester. As the Quiet Woman was still open, they called in.

The bar became quiet as they walked through it, but Betty held her head high. As before, the friends sat in the snug, but they were subdued.

Charlie looked sad.

'We never even caught the Stocking Stealer.'

'Things seem to have been quiet over the past few weeks,' Betty said. 'Maybe whoever it was has given up.'

'I reckon they realised we're on to them,' a voice came from the bar. It was Herbie Potter. 'So they've stopped. Of course, if people didn't tip off the suspects . . .'

Betty would have spoken, but a commotion in the bar stopped her.

'I need to speak to Betty, please!'

She stood up and went to the snug door.

'Rosie, what is it?'

'Daisy's gone! I tried to stop her, but she's gone with Harry to Blackpool. She says they're going to get married!'

'Daisy?'

Rosie nodded.

'You have to bring her back, please!'

'I will, sweetheart. How long has she been gone?'

'About half an hour.'

Betty turned to her father.

'Dad, can I use the car?'

'Of course, love. Do you want me to come with you?'

'I'll go,' Ben, who had followed Betty to the snug door, said. 'I think I know where they might have gone, and the hotel in Blackpool he might have taken her to.'

He and Charlie exchanged knowing glances.

'We hear talk.'

'I'll come with you,' Rosie cried.

'I think you should stay here with me and Tom,' Maggie said. 'It could be hours. Let Betty and Ben bring her back.'

Ben and Betty went around to the back of the pub, where Tom kept the family car. Ben put the keys in the ignition and turned. Nothing. He tried again. Nothing still.

'Now, I wonder what could be wrong with this,' he said in a tired voice. A few moments' investigation showed that the rotor arm was missing.

They had no choice but to go back into the pub.

'The rotor arm has gone,' Betty said, loud enough for everyone to hear. 'And as Dad dropped us off in Shrewsbury to go to the pictures, Ben can't have done it. He was with us the whole time.'

The bar fell silent.

'Look here.' Ben addressed everyone. 'You may not like me, but there's a young girl who's got herself into a

190

difficult situation. We need to get to her before anything happens to her. You know what I'm talking about. She's just a kid and probably doesn't realise how serious this is. But the guy she's with, I hear this isn't the first time he's done it. So please, someone help us.'

'You can take the post van.'

Herbie Potter stood up and took the keys out of his pocket.

'It's parked up at my cottage. Watch out for that clutch. It's a bit dickey, but it should get you to Blackpool. There ought to be enough petrol.'

'Take some from mine, just in case,' Tom said.

'You're going to have problems with the curfew. You'd best square it with the Home Guard.'

By the time everything was organised, half an hour had passed.

'How would he be able to beat the curfew?' Betty asked Ben as they drove along the darkened roads towards the North West of England.

'Probably got a three-day pass. He

can go pretty much anywhere with that.'

'Poor, silly, Daisy. I hope we're not too late, Ben.'

* * *

It might have seemed inappropriate, but that drive up to Blackpool was one of the happiest few hours of Betty's life. She and Ben were able to talk to each other without interruption for the first time ever. They still avoided certain subjects, like Ben's leaving and Eddie, but it was nice to be together.

It felt like they had the whole world to themselves as they drove along the darkened roads, illuminated only by the dimmed headlights. There were a couple of scary moments, when they heard bombers way above them. When that happened, Ben pulled over to the side.

'If it's taken us this long, it would have taken Harry as long,' Ben pointed out. 'We may catch up with them yet.'

When they reached Blackpool there was hardly anyone around, apart from the air raid wardens, so the hotel took some finding. When they did find it, the landlady, was disgruntled to be woken. She was an overblown, heavily made-up lady in her late forties.

'I don't run that type of establishment,' she huffed.

'There's a young girl who needs to be back with her sister,' Betty pleaded. 'She's only sixteen. Surely you'd notice someone that young.'

'There's a war on, love. They all look young to me.'

'She was with an American by the name of Harry. He plays in a band. He often brings women here.'

'I've already said, this is a respectable establishment.' The landlady licked her thin lips. 'But sometimes I . . . charge double to look the other way.'

'So exactly how much did Harry pay you to look the other way?'

'OK. But he's not here. I mean he was, but he left.'

'What about the girl, Daisy?' Betty felt an icy finger down her spine.

'She left soon after. Crying, she was.'

'You let her go off alone into the night?'

'I'm not her keeper! People can come and go as they please, as long as they pay their bill.' She looked at them shrewdly. 'So, how about you two?'

'No,' Ben told her. 'We don't want a room. If we ever come back to Blackpool and stay in a hotel, it will be as a legally married couple.'

They stepped outside into the night. Betty's head was reeling — first about Daisy being missing, and then about what Ben had said.

She knew he was only making a point, but for a moment the thought had been a wonderful one.

'What are we going to do, Ben?' she asked. 'Blackpool is a big place. How can we ever find Daisy?'

'Betty! Is that really you?'

She spun around and saw a slight figure in the distance, illuminated by the moon.

'Daisy?'

The girl ran to them and fell sobbing into Betty's arms.

'Oh, I've been so stupid, Betty!'

In For Questioning

'Nothing happened, honest, Betty. I really thought we were going to get married. Then, when we got to the room, he started going on about how marriage was outdated and we didn't need that if we loved each other.'

Daisy took a deep, shaky breath.

'I'm not that stupid, Betty, even though I wouldn't blame you for thinking so, after what I did. I told him no, and he just left me there. I was afraid on my own, so I went to a club where he goes to play, to ask him to take me back to Midchester. Would you believe he already had some other girl lined up?' She burst into tears again.

Daisy sat on the seat between them in the post van as they drove back to Midchester in the early hours of the morning.

'Everyone is going to be so angry

with me, aren't they?'

'Don't worry about it, kid. Everyone is entitled to make one mistake when they're your age. And it sounds to me as though that head is screwed on pretty good. We'll make sure everyone knows that.'

Betty blessed Ben for saying it.

'Your friends know the truth,' Betty squeezed her hand.

'As for Harry, I'll speak to his commanding officer about him.'

With the resilience of youth, Daisy had cheered up somewhat by the time they pulled up outside Herbie's cottage. Ben put the keys through the letterbox, and they all walked back to the pub together.

Maggie was asleep on the sofa, and Tom had fallen asleep reading the newspaper on his favourite armchair. Rosie came hurtling from Betty's bedroom the moment Betty, Ben and Daisy wearily climbed the stairs to the pub living quarters.

'Oh, Daisy, you idiot! I was so

worried. Don't ever do that to me again.'

'I won't, I promise.' Daisy hugged her sister.

'Is everything all right?' Tom asked.

'Daisy was very sensible.' Betty's meaning was clear.

Tom breathed a big sigh of relief.

About half an hour later, there was a loud knock on the pub door. Tom went to answer it.

'Is Captain Benedict Greenwood here?'

'Why, yes, he's upstairs.' A few moments later, Tom appeared upstairs with a man dressed in an American airman's uniform.

'Air Admiral O'Brian!' Ben stood up.

'Captain Greenwood — Ben — please come with me.'

'What's wrong, Sir?'

'It's ridiculous, Ben, but there have been reports you've been consorting with the enemy. We've just taken a Professor Solomon in for questioning.'

'Am I under arrest, Sir?'

'No, Captain. That's why I came myself. I'm sure we'll sort this out, but we can't ignore it. This morning a load of vehicles up at the airbase were tampered with.'

'Let me guess,' Ben said. 'The rotor arms went missing.'

'It can't have been Ben. He was with me,' Betty said. Her face burned scarlet when she saw the look on the air admiral's face. 'We had to drive to Blackpool.'

'It's true,' Daisy said. 'They came to fetch me back after I'd done something silly. Ben's a good guy.'

'So is the professor!' Rosie had tears in her eyes.

'I'm sure we'll find it's a misunderstanding, miss.'

'Strange things have been happening, though,' Betty said. 'Stockings stolen off lines, chocolate taken from larders, rotor arms going missing.'

'Was all this reported to the police?' O'Brian asked.

'Well, no, it didn't seem important.

We thought it might just be children.'

'We'll look into it now, miss. We can't have one of our country's heroes accused of espionage. Come on, Greenwood, we need you back so we can sort out this mess.'

The morning that followed was interminable for Betty. Her father insisted she try to sleep after her night of travelling, but she was too worried. Working behind the bar at lunch time did not help. The whole village knew about the professor being arrested and Ben being taken away for questioning.

'I don't know what my Eddie would say if he were here,' Mrs Simpson said pointedly on more than one occasion.

Betty did her best to ignore it.

'They'll be wanting to talk to everyone who made friends with them, I reckon,' Len Simpson said from his corner. 'Not that we haven't warned certain people.'

Betty switched him off in her head and got on with her work, remembering to smile at the customers and tidy away the glasses.

'Look at them,' Peg muttered from her seat. 'Vultures picking at the carcass before the animal is even dead.'

'They'll be all right, I know it.' She said it as much to assure herself as Peg.

'If they're not, then this world really is upside down.'

Someone else entered the pub, and had to be regaled with the story of the arrests. Betty only vaguely heard the telephone ring and saw Maggie answer it.

'Betty?' Maggie broke into Betty's thoughts. 'Sorry, pet, but do you mind if I go early? I've just had a telephone call from Herbie. He's come down with something and wants me to go over for an hour or two.'

'Then you must go. Do thank him for the use of the van last night. I haven't had a chance, with everything that's been happening. I hope he feels better soon.'

The rest of the day dragged on with

no news of Ben or the professor. Charlie and Fiona came down to the pub for evening opening.

'Any news?' Betty asked eagerly.

Charlie shook his head.

'No. Ben hasn't come back to Bedlington Hall, either.'

'It's been hours now! They surely can't keep them that long when there's no evidence against them.'

'They can do what they want in a war, Betty,'

Not long after that, Daisy and Rosie arrived, and sat in the snug with Charlie and Fiona, drinking lemonade.

'Mr Armstrong almost dismissed me,' Daisy told them. 'But he changed his mind when I told him what had happened. He said I was daft, but he'd let me off this time.'

'Just try and keep out of trouble for a bit.' Betty smiled.

The evening topic of conversation was the arrest of Ben and the professor. The customers appeared to find them both guilty, without a scrap of evidence.

Betty could only hope that the people interviewing Ben and the professor were a little more balanced in their deliberations.

'The pub is doing well,' Tom muttered at one point, 'but I'm not sure I like making money this way.'

'Me, neither.'

Time wore on and there was no sign of Ben or the professor. It was about ten o'clock when Rachel Solomon came into the pub. The whole room went quiet, but she walked through them all with her chin up.

'Rachel! I'm so glad you're back.' Betty lifted the flap on the counter and took Rachel's arm in a friendly gesture meant for the whole pub to see.

'I just wanted you to know that my father is in hospital, not in prison.' She spoke in a loud, clear voice.

'Hospital?'

'Yes. He was taken ill during questioning.'

Tom spoke first.

'What on earth did they do to him?'

'Nothing. They were very courteous with both of us. But my father is a good, proud man, and he has come to love this country. The strain of being accused of such a thing upset him greatly, and after a while he started to get pains in his chest. They took him to Shrewsbury. Ben drove the ambulance himself, and he has insisted on staying with Papa. I've come to collect some clothes for my father, and then I will return to him. I have to catch the last bus back.'

'No,' Tom said. 'My car is mended, so I'll take you back there. Betty, can you close up, love?'

'Of course, Dad. I'll get the twins to help me clear up.'

Tom left with Rachel soon after. Betty stood in the middle of the bar looking at the customers, all of whom were finding the contents of their glasses very interesting.

It was with some relief later that Betty locked the pub door. Charlie, Fiona and the twins stayed behind to help her clear up.

'I shouldn't be keeping you girls here,' she said to Daisy and Rosie. 'You have to be up early in the morning.'

'We want to know what happens with Ben and the professor,' Rosie said.

They all sat in the living-room, listening to the clock ticking.

'If we could just find out who's really doing it,' said Fiona, as Betty handed her a cup of tea.

'We got nowhere,' Betty said ruefully. 'It was always the same thing. People got up in the morning, did their chores, read their post and then — '

'What is it?' Charlie demanded. 'You're on to something. I can see it in your eyes.'

'I don't know.' Betty shrugged. 'It's just something I heard so many times that I'm beginning to wonder if it actually means something.' She shook her head. If her suspicions were right, it did not make much sense. 'I don't want to go pointing the finger at someone or I'd be no better than everyone in the pub tonight.'

'I notice there was no sign of the Simpsons,' Fiona said.

'Nor Peg, for that matter. That's odd. She normally comes in, if only for one drink.' Betty frowned. 'Maggie said Herbie had come down with something. What if Peg has, too? I think I'll go and check on her.'

'We'll come part of the way with you.' Daisy yawned. 'Then Rosie and I will head back to the farm.'

'But we'll come down at lunchtime tomorrow for news of Ben and the professor,' her sister said.

'We'd best be heading back, too,' Fiona said. 'Come on, Charlie.'

They all left with Betty, and she locked up, leaving the key under a plant pot for her father to find just in case he returned whilst she was away. She had no fear of walking back in the dark. She knew Midchester too well for that.

She left her friends at the crossroads and went on to Peg's house, shivering slightly in the cool night air. Walking out in the dark alone had seemed like a good idea, but before the war, there would have been lights in every window. Since the war, everyone had blackout blinds, and the buildings loomed dark against the night sky, showing little light and comfort for the traveller.

Betty hesitated before knocking quietly on Peg's door. It opened a few minutes later, and Peg peered out, holding a handkerchief to her nose.

'Oh, hello, Betty, dear.'

'Sorry, Peg. I was just worried about you.'

'I've caught a cold, so thought I'd stay at home so as not to spread it about.' Peg sniffed as if to make her point.

'I think Herbie Potter has the same thing,' said Betty. 'Maggie has been off all day tending to him.'

'Men do make a meal of these things. For me a tot of whisky and some warm broth is enough. You should get off back home in the warm before you catch something, dear.'

'It's not really cold, Peg. I'm fine.'

'Do you want to come in for a cup of tea?' The question was half-hearted, and it occurred to Betty that Peg definitely was not her usual self. It was with surprise she realised Peg was deliberately keeping her on the door-step.

'No, it's fine. I'll go home. Dad should be back soon.'

'Where's he been?'

Betty quickly told Peg about the professor and Ben.

'Rachel said her father collapsed during the questioning. Hardly surprising considering what they've already been through.'

'I do hope he'll be OK,' Peg said. 'I also hope people will be more careful about casting accusations in future.'

'I hope you feel better soon, Peg. I'll call in and see you with some soup tomorrow.'

'You're a good girl. Don't let anyone tell you different.'

There was more that Peg was not saying, but all Betty could do was wave goodnight. On the walk home her head spun with everything that had happened over the past weeks.

It all seemed to have led to this point. Even Daisy's dash to Blackpool seemed linked in some way that Betty could not put her finger on, along with Peg and Herbie's sudden simultaneous illnesses. She thought back over the previous days, trying to capture the memory of one look, one word, one action that would give her the answer.

As she neared the pub she saw a figure in the shadows.

'Who is it?' she called, trembling slightly.

'It's only me.'

'Ben!'

Relieved to see him after so much uncertainty, Betty ran into his arms, welcoming the kiss he gave.

The Culprit Found

They sat on the sofa in the upstairs living-room, holding hands. Her father had gone up to bed, realising that they would want to be alone for a while.

'Was it dreadful?'

'The kiss? I thought it was great!'

'I meant was it dreadful being questioned?'

'Not for me.' Ben's voice became grim. 'I had nothing to prove. But the professor seemed shaken up by it.'

'Because he's suffered persecution before.'

Ben nodded.

'I'm so darn angry with those who put him through it again. I don't care for myself, Betty. I'm young enough to let such things flow over me. But he felt it deeply.'

'Will he have to face questioning again?'

'No. They've been through his cottage. There's no secret radio, no notes in cypher. Unless he's using the Roman invasion of Britain as a metaphor for the German invasion!' He smiled, but it didn't quite reach his eyes.

'I think I might know who's been doing it, Ben. Stealing the stockings and the rotor arms, I mean. I was thinking about it on the way home from Peg's tonight, and how things are all connected. It's hard to explain, and nothing is certain.'

'Just a hunch, eh?'

'That's it exactly. A hunch.'

'Who do you think it is?'

'I'd rather not tell you. If I'm wrong, then it's a dreadful mistake. I need proof.'

'What can I do to help?'

'I think, for your sake, you have to keep out of this. It might be seen as an attempt to clear your name by blaming someone else. If I'm right, this is exactly what this person has been doing. I see how it all started now — the gossip going around that no-one claims to have started. The insistence it was a fifth columnist. It made me think, who has access to that many villagers? The one person who could so easily say 'I've just heard', and then no-one could say for sure who started the rumours.'

'You've lost me completely.'

'I think I've just found you.' Betty stroked his cheek.

They kissed again, and all too soon it was time to say goodnight.

'I wish you'd let me help you,' Ben said, as they stood at the door. 'I'm afraid you'll be in danger.'

Betty shook her head.

'None of the crimes committed have hurt anyone. Not really. It's only inconvenienced them.'

'Professor Solomon might disagree with that.'

'Of course. I'm sorry, Ben, I didn't mean that. What I mean is that the perpetrator hasn't personally hurt someone physically, and I don't think they will.'

'OK. I'll see you tomorrow.'

*   *   *

She put her head on her pillow and when she opened her eyes it was daylight. Jumping out of bed with a gasp of horror, she dressed and dashed downstairs. Her father was down in the cellar.

'Sorry I slept late, Dad!'

'Don't you worry about it,' Tom said. 'I let you sleep in. You've had a busy couple of days. Get some breakfast.'

'Any news from Maggie?'

'No. I tried to telephone her last night, but there was no answer at her house. I tried Herbie's too, but no-one was answering there, so I imagine they were asleep.'

The next hour or so was spent in rolling casks down into the cellar, and putting bottle ales on the shelves, after wiping them with a cloth to remove the dust from the road.

There was no sign of Peg, Herbie, Maggie or the Simpsons during the afternoon session. The bar seemed strangely empty and quiet without them.

'They must have all come down with something,' said Tom, when there were no customers and a quiet moment to chat. 'I've tried Maggie again this morning but she's not answering.'

'I'm taking some soup to Peg and Herbie this afternoon, Dad. I'll find out what's wrong.'

'Thanks, love. Herbie doesn't really approve of me seeing Maggie.'

'He's wrong. You're perfect for each other.'

'How would you feel about me getting married again?'

'I think it would be wonderful!' Betty beamed.

'Hold on, I haven't asked her yet. I just wanted to see how you felt about it first. I don't want you to think I'm replacing your mum. I loved her more than anything, Betty. That love will never die just because I love Maggie now.'

'I know that, Dad. There's room in that big heart of yours for lots of love. Maggie is a lucky woman and I shall tell her that when I see her.'

'I hope she agrees with you.'

'She'd be a fool not to.'

After closing time, Betty and her dad ate some of the soup she'd made that morning, and she put the rest into covered dishes for Peg and Herbie. She felt guilty knowing that at least one of them was just a ruse to get in and ask questions, but she carried on regardless.

Her first stop was at Peg's. Peg invited her into the living-room, but Betty noticed Peg would not look her in the eye. Nor did Peg appear to have the cold she claimed to have had the night before. Her eyes were swollen, as if she had been crying, but that was all.

'How are you feeling?' Betty asked cheerfully.

'A little better, thank you, Betty, dear.'

'I've brought some chicken soup for you, Peg. You've probably had lunch, but you can heat it up later.'

'That's very kind. Would you like a cup of tea?'

'I can't stop, I'm off to Herbie's with this other pot.'

'Betty — '

'Yes?'

'Don't go to Herbie's. I don't think he wants visitors.'

'I'll just drop it off. Besides, Dad is a bit worried about Maggie. He's been trying to contact her.'

'I think she's a bit indisposed at the moment, taking care of Herbie. Best leave them to it.'

That was when it dawned on Betty.

'You know, don't you?' she whispered. 'Maggie knows, too. But you worked it out before I did!'

'Yes . . . no. I don't know. Perhaps we realised at the same time.'

'Why didn't you tell anyone?'

'He's one of us, Betty. A Midchester lad.'

'That's no excuse.' Tears were stinging her eyes. 'Ben was suspected. The professor was arrested and is ill in hospital as a result. Two innocent men might have suffered even more, had the Air Admiral not used common sense.'

'But now they're both free. I've checked, and the Air Admiral assured me that no further charges will be made against Ben or the professor. So we just need to keep this to ourselves. Nothing else will happen, and the Stocking Stealer won't steal stockings or rotor arms again.'

'No!' Betty cried. 'It can't be swept under the carpet like that. It can't!' She looked at Peg aghast. 'I thought I knew you, Peg, but now I'm not so sure.'

She had always relied on Peg to be honest, and stand up for justice.

'Justice is a strange concept,' Peg said as if reading Betty's mind. 'Sometimes it does hurt innocent people, and sometimes even those who are guilty aren't blamed as much as one might think. It's like you and Eddie scrumping apples. Of course it's stealing, but . . . '

'We were kids, we knew no better. He's a grown man.'

'So he must always behave with common sense and fortitude? I'm afraid human beings are never quite as perfect as that.' Peg's voice became sad. 'The man I loved a very long time ago now, murdered his own father. Everyone was against him, and so was I, until I learned what had been done to him as a child by the father who should have protected him. He still took his punishment when it was meted out. He swore me to secrecy.'

'Peg, I'm sorry about the man you loved, and I wish there had been someone to help him when he needed it. But lots of people are suffering in this war. They've lost loved ones, or been hurt themselves. They've seen all sorts of horrors. But that doesn't mean they all get to do what they want. Look at Charlie Turner. He suffers dreadfully for the things he's seen, and yet he wouldn't harm a living soul.' Betty shook her head vigorously as she spoke.

'Mrs Baker is alone with five children, struggling day by day, and everyone looks down on her. Yet she manages to be honest and not hurt anyone. No, Peg, I don't believe you undo the wrong that's been done to you by doing wrong to others.'

Unable to bear any more, Betty turned and fled the cottage, with Peg's entreaties echoing in her ears. She surged through Midchester to Herbie's cottage near to the small train station.

Herbie's home was in a row of a dozen railway cottages that opened straight out onto the street, with long back gardens behind, leading down to the railway lines. As with most of the gardens in Midchester, access along the back was open to anyone who wanted to take a short cut. Something which Betty now knew Herbie had taken great advantage of.

The post van was parked outside and she idly wondered who delivered the post that morning, if Herbie didn't. As far as she could remember, no mail had come to the pub.

Maggie's house was at the other end of the row. She hammered on the door, but it swung open. Without waiting for an invitation, Betty stormed in, and came to a sudden halt when she saw her father standing in front of the fireplace in the small parlour. He had his arm around Maggie, who was crying.

'Dad?'

'Betty, love, sit down and listen.'

'No, you listen. I worked it out. Everyone said the same thing you see . . . '

'Betty,' Maggie entreated.

'I know what happened,' Tom said. 'Maggie telephoned me after you left and asked me to come over.'

'They all said they'd done their chores then stopped to read their post,' Betty continued. 'That's what everyone does now the war is on, because everyone is waiting for news of loved ones. The whole village stops to find out what's happening in the world via all those letters and cards. That was when Herbie took the stockings and tampered with the cars.'

'Betty!' Her dad held his hand up in supplication.

'Then he did something even more unforgiveable,' Betty continued, determined not to be side-lined. 'He started the rumours about the fifth columnist, though he let Len Simpson be the one to say it in public. I imagine he also went from house to house, telling people what others were supposed to have said, when it all really came from him. Herbie let Ben and the professor be blamed for it all. Now the professor is ill . . . '

'It's made Herbie ill, too, Betty,' Maggie cried. 'He's been in his bed since yesterday. He's tried to make amends. He gave Mrs Baker a new pair of stockings, and he lent you and Ben the post van when he realised young Daisy might be in danger. He's not all bad, Betty.'

'That'll only be his conscience,' Betty snapped. She could hardly believe that people were making excuses for Herbie Potter after all he had done. 'Herbie isn't even forty yet. The professor must be nearer to seventy. His recovery is not so certain. The only thing I don't understand is, why?'

'This is what we're trying to tell you, if you'll just listen,' her father said. 'His lady friend, Floss, left him for that musician, Harry. They went off to that same hotel in Blackpool! Now there's a baby involved. That's why Floss is at her sister's, because she knew she couldn't come back here as an unmarried mother.'

Betty felt a pang of sadness, remembering how she had worried the same might happen to Daisy.

'Herbie had it in for the American airmen from then on. That's why he stole the stockings.'

'When you started asking questions,' Maggie said, taking up the story, 'he started on the cars, so people would think it was a fifth columnist. Peg worked it out and confronted him yesterday. That's why he telephoned me.'

'He's promised to stop now,' Tom said. 'When he heard about the professor being taken ill he realised what pain he had caused innocent people.'

'You're not suggesting he just gets away with it, Dad?'

'He's one of us, Betty.'

'And Ben and the professor aren't. Is that how it works? It doesn't matter what pain you cause to outsiders, because the village will cover it all up?'

'People will find out, Betty,' Maggie said. 'It's inevitable. But we don't want to send one of our own to prison. Of course, it's up to you whether you tell, love.'

A tear rolled down Betty's cheek.

'That's not fair. If I tell, then every-one is going to hate me. Especially you,

Maggie, because he's your brother.'

'No-one will hate you, love.'

'Yes, they will. It's a pity Herbie didn't think to look after his own, instead of turning against them all! Because he hurt the village, too. For a start, he stole the stockings and tampered with the vehicles of his neighbours, not the airmen. Then when he started the rumours about the fifth columnist, he brought out the very worst in human nature.

'I've seen a side to my neighbours I never thought to see. I've seen them persecute an elderly man who has already suffered enough pain in his life. I've seen them stick their noses up at a young man who nearly died fighting for this country. I'll never be able to think the same of Midchester again. Never!'

She turned and fled Herbie's house in a fit of sobbing.

As she went through the village, not entirely sure where she was going, Betty began to wonder why she had ever worried about what people would think about her and Ben if Herbie could get away with doing much worse. She and Ben were two young, unmarried people who liked each other.

She made up her mind in that moment to go and tell Ben that she loved him. It didn't matter what anyone else thought any more. If they gossiped, so be it. Obviously some people were forgiven more than others in Midchester. Herbie was protected, whilst poor Floss, who had made a silly mistake over a man, dare not return to her home village with her baby. It was double standards, Betty fumed as she dashed through the village.

Betty neared the church gate, determined to take the path up to Bedlington Hall and see Ben. She was just opening the gate, her head down, deep in thought when she bumped straight into Mrs Simpson.

'Hello,' she said curtly. She certainly wasn't in the mood for her today.

'Hello, Betty, dear. I was going to come see you soon.'

'What about?'

Mrs Simpson's voice had the same placatory tones that her father, Peg and Maggie had had over Herbie Potter, along with an unwillingness to look Betty in the eye. She probably knew about Herbie, too, and no doubt would give Betty another lesson in forgiveness.

'You've probably been wondering where we were.'

'What? Oh, yes, of course. I noticed you haven't been in the pub for a day or two.'

'We've been down to London.' Mrs Simpson caught Betty's arms with her hands and her face broke out into an elated smile. 'To see Eddie!'

'Eddie?' Betty felt the ground give way under her.

'He's alive, Betty. Eddie is alive!'

Return To The Battle

The first thing Betty needed to do was sit down. She went to the church porch and plonked herself on a seat.

'It's wonderful news!' she said to Mrs Simpson, and she meant every word. Whatever else had happened in her life, she had never wished any harm to Eddie.

'I knew it all along. A mother knows these things, you see.'

There was only a small note of triumph in Mrs Simpson's voice. She sat next to Betty, still giving the impression that she did not want to look her in the eye. But Betty's own emotions were so mixed, she pushed the thought aside.

'Where has he been?'

'In a prisoner-of-war camp. Only he'd lost his memory and his identification after being injured, so no-one knew who he was. It's only recently that his memory has returned. Then, as soon as he remembered his name and rank, they — what was the word? They repatriated him, that's it. They sent him home via Switzerland. He's been there about six weeks, waiting for a flight to Lisbon then a boat home. We only got the call yesterday to go down to London and see him. He's in a big hospital there.'

'When is he coming home?'

'Well . . . ' Myrtle hesitated, and not for the first time over the past few hours, Betty had a feeling of things not being said. 'We're not quite sure yet. The doctors will let us know when they've assessed him properly. I've only popped home to get a few things and tell everyone. We're going down to stay with my cousin in Chelsea for a few days so we can keep going to the hospital.'

'I'll come down with you to see him,' Betty offered. 'Just for the day, I mean.'

She needed to speak to Eddie, to put

things straight. But first she needed to know how bad he was.

'Oh, no, I don't think they're allowing anyone other than family in at the moment. No, you'd best stay here. I'm sure he'll want to see you when he's well.'

Myrtle didn't sound very sure at all, but Betty put it down to a mother's possessiveness. It was natural she should want to keep her son to herself after two years of not knowing if he were dead or alive. It made Betty ashamed for the times she had been impatient with Mrs. Simpson for interfering in her life.

Perhaps it was true, and a mother did know these things better than anyone else.

At that moment Betty missed the wise counsel of her own mother, who would have known how to sort all the problems out. She could not rely on her dad any more, nor Peg or Maggie. At that moment she felt more alone than ever before.

She could not even continue with her plan to speak to Ben. At least not in the way she wanted to. With Eddie alive, her promise still stood and, until she could speak to Eddie and sort things out, so that a line was drawn under the past, she could not move on. Who knew what affect that might have on him in his injured state? She did not want to strike a blow to someone who was already fragile.

'Very well, I'll wait till he comes back to Midchester. I suppose I'd better be going. I need to sort some things out.' Impulsively Betty kissed Mrs Simpson on the cheek, much to the lady's surprise. 'I'm glad Eddie is alive, really I am.'

And it was true. It might make her life more complicated, but it was welcome news in a world where there was precious little to be glad about.

Betty took the path up to Bedlington Hall, but with less purpose than before. She wanted to tell Ben about Eddie, but she could not really admit her feelings to Ben when she was still promised to another man. It would not be right.

When she reached the hospital, she saw several trucks outside, and a flurry of activity as men were loaded onto them.

'What's going on?' she asked one of the nurses.

'They've called them all back. All those who are able, that is. Though that's a matter of opinion. The doctor is not pleased at all, but he has been overruled. The top brass don't care about these boys at all, if you ask me.' The nurse went about her business of helping men into the wagons.

Betty made her way to the front entrance and had just reached it when Ben came out with his kit bag over his shoulder, surrounded by other airmen, including Charlie.

'Hello, Betty. Goodbye, Betty!' Charlie waved to her. His red-rimmed eyes suggested that he had already said his goodbyes to Fiona.

Betty guessed she was inside some-where, drying her own tears.

'Hey, Betty.' Ben smiled, but his face looked strained.

'You were going to leave without telling me?'

'I wanted to come and tell you,' he replied, 'but I've been ordered not to leave the hospital unless it's in one of those trucks. I can't disobey an order, Betty. I asked Fiona to tell you.'

So that was it. No note, only a second-hand message via a friend.

'But you'll only be going to the airfield, won't you?'

Ben shook his head.

'We're going further away than that, so we're nearer to the Front. I can't tell you where. I wish I could, but it's classified.'

'You're really going back to fight?'

'I am. It's where I want to be.' He looked around him. 'Actually, this is where I want to be, but over there is where I have to be. Anyway, what brought you up here?'

'I needed to tell you something.'

'What's that?'

There were so many things to say, Betty hardly knew where to start.

'I know who the Stocking Stealer is.'

It put off the inevitable news about Eddie, but it was all she could manage to say, under the weight of Ben's parting.

'Yeah, it was Herbie, the postman.'

'You knew?'

Betty began to wonder if all of England knew that Herbie was the stocking stealer, and she was the only one who had been wandering around with her eyes shut for the past few weeks.

'I only found out this morning. He was seen on the airfield the night the vehicles were tampered with. Some of the guys remembered him going up there drunk on the night when his girl ran off with Harry, and so they put two and two together.'

'So why hasn't the Air Admiral had Herbie arrested?'

'He didn't harm any military vehicles, otherwise he might have. Besides, there's enough bad feeling because of Harry's behaviour. The Air Admiral decided we didn't need to start picking on the locals.'

'But picking on the professor was all right?'

Betty could hardly believe her ears. Even Ben seemed to be covering up for Herbie.

'Of course it wasn't, Betty, and he's going to receive a full apology.'

'Let's hope he lives long enough to hear it,' Betty said savagely.

'What's really wrong?' Ben frowned after looking at her for a long hard moment. 'This is not just about Herbie, is it?'

Betty swallowed hard.

'No, it isn't. I was on my way up to see you to . . . just to see you.'

Now that Eddie loomed between them again, she could not say what she really wanted to. That and the fact that she felt at that moment that Ben had let her down, just like her father, Maggie and Peg.

'I saw Mrs Simpson.'

'Is she reminding you of your promise to Eddie again?'

'In a manner of speaking, yes.'

Betty's lips felt dry. She swallowed again, but her mouth seemed to be lined with sandpaper.

'Eddie's alive.'

Ben's eyes widened.

'Is she sure?'

'She's seen him. She went down to London yesterday. He's in a hospital there, but he'll be coming home soon.'

That was not exactly what Mrs Simpson said, but it was close enough.

'I see.'

'So I need to see him. To sort things out.'

'Do you?'

'Yes, of course. He's been badly hurt and he lost his memory, but now it's coming back.'

'So, you're ready to sacrifice your own happiness for that of the conquering hero, eh?' She saw the muscle in Ben's cheek contract, as if he were struggling to hold his temper.

'That's a dreadful thing to say, Ben! I just have to draw a line under the past, before I can move on. That's what I'm saying. Until I know how bad Eddie is — well, you wouldn't kick a man when he's down, would you?'

'Is that so? Because it sure feels that way at the moment.'

'What do you mean?' She was about to remind him that he was planning to leave without saying goodbye, but that sounded petty even to her.

'Nothing, Betty. Nothing. I shouldn't have even said it. You've had enough people telling you what to do and how you should feel. I don't want to be one of them.'

A shout came up from the group of people. They were ready to move out and only Ben held them up.

'I guess this is it. Take care of yourself, kid.'

'Yes. You too.'

She looked up at him, wishing she could kiss him goodbye, but there seemed to be a ten-foot wall called Eddie between them again.

'I mean it, Ben. Take care. And — come back, please.'

Ben didn't reply. He just walked away from her and threw his things into a truck before climbing up next to Charlie. She wanted to run after him, to tell him all that was in her heart, but his coldness stopped her.

Perhaps she had only been a fling for him, which was why it was so easy for him to leave without saying goodbye. Maybe when she allowed him to kiss her had been enough for him to know he had succeeded in wooing her after her initial caution.

He hadn't said he would write to her, and she had no idea how to contact him, though she supposed she could ask Fiona, who would most certainly write to Charlie.

'I hope things work out for you and

Eddie!' he called as the truck started to move away.

'No, Ben, listen!' she called, running after the truck, but it was too late. The truck gathered speed and rolled down the hill. She watched it until it was out of sight. Only then did she break down in tears.

★   ★   ★

Betty could never remember how she got through the next few months. Somehow, despite her heartache she managed to get up every morning and put one foot in front of the other. She was able to smile when she was expected to, and engage in polite conversation when the occasion arose; which was often in the pub.

But things were not the same. She was not the same. And she could no longer look at her friends and neighbours in the same way. They had disappointed her. It was apparent in their apologetic eyes when they spoke to her that they realised it, no matter how much she tried to put a brave face on things.

Gradually Herbie started coming into the pub as if nothing had happened, and whilst things were tense at first — the word of his wrongdoing had spread around the village — soon it was as if nothing had happened. He was one of them, after all. Rumour started that he was walking out with Mrs Baker, and not long after that she started to accompany him to the pub on the nights she could get a babysitter. There was talk of them marrying sometime in the future, and though the gossips did not exactly approve, there was a sense that two of the village's problems were to be sorted out in one fell swoop.

'A woman needs a husband to keep her in check,' Mrs Simpson told her friends.

Peg sat on her same stool, although she was quieter than she used to be, and Maggie took up her place in the bar at night-time. All other talk was about Tom and Maggie's planned marriage, and that helped to keep the discussion away from more painful subjects. What Betty saw as their betrayal was something which hung heavy in the atmosphere, but which was never alluded to.

On the days Betty helped on the farm, she dug until she was exhausted, even though it did not do much to help her sleep. At night she scoured the newspaper or listened to the radio for news of any action by the air force, and then sat down in her bedroom and wrote letters to Ben, all of which she ripped up and threw into the fire. She did not know what to say to him after the manner of their parting. Eddie still had not returned home, so her life became as static as it had been when she was waiting for him before Ben arrived in Midchester.

The Simpsons seemed to be avoiding her, for reasons she did not quite understand. She thought at first that they were still angry about Ben, but that did not seem to be it. They were civil enough when they saw her. Affectionate, even! Sometimes she even thought they seemed apologetic, but could not put her finger on why.

All she knew was that, apart from ordering drinks from her, they seemed to avoid any other conversation, especially that which might lead to discussing Eddie. Betty began to wonder if he were worse than Mrs Simpson had said, and she was afraid to let on.

'Do you write to that young airman?' Len Simpson asked Betty one day after he had ordered his drink.

She shook her head.

'No. His friend, Charlie, writes to Fiona, but Ben is out of the picture.'

'Well,' Len demurred, 'there's no real harm in two young people being friends, is there?'

Surprised, and fearing a trap of some sort, Betty just smiled.

'Well, that's all over now.'

The twins, Daisy and Rosie were

always at the farm when she went there, and they were touchingly mindful of Betty's feelings and comfort. It occurred to her that they were the only ones, besides Professor Solomon and Rachel who hadn't let her down. They brought Betty little treats they had made during their time off, like cakes and sweets. Sometimes they insisted on doing her work at the farm for her, even though she did not allow that too often.

Whenever they could they went with Betty to Professor Solomon's dig, where they all helped because he was not yet well enough to do the heavy work himself. Between them, the three girls learned how to excavate an archaeological site properly, and to catalogue their finds.

They attended his talks, mainly because few of the villagers did, apart from some servicemen and nurses from the hospital. Even though the professor had been exonerated, the villagers avoided him. Betty guessed it was out of shame, rather than because they still distrusted him. Occasionally she went with the twins and Fiona to the pictures. Other times she went on long walks on her own.

In this way Betty filled her life as much as she could, because she was afraid that, if she sat down and thought too long, she would start to cry over Ben again. She veered from believing he was all things wonderful, to believing he was probably no better than Harry the musician in the way he played with her heart.

Fiona received letters from Charlie, but being Charlie they were full of silly jokes, which said very little about how he or Ben were really getting on.

'For Charlie, humour is a coping mechanism,' Fiona explained when they went to the pictures one night. 'It gets annoying sometimes, but he jokes so that he doesn't have to start talking about how he really feels.'

'Isn't that just being a man?' Betty suggested with a sad smile.

'Actually, now you come to mention it, yes!'

'Is . . . is Ben all right?'

'Charlie says he is. Though he says he doesn't see him much either. Ben is the first one to volunteer for missions. Charlie said it's almost like he has a — ' Fiona bit her lip. Betty didn't ask her to finish the sentence because she was afraid to hear it. 'He's very brave, Ben is. Charlie is, too, though he feels things more deeply. Not that you'd know it from his letters!'

'Tell him I said hello next time you write,' Betty said. She wanted to add a message for Ben, too, but as she didn't have the courage to write to him personally it felt wrong to ask Fiona to pass on her messages.

Even if that's what he had intended to do on the day he left Midchester.

'He really had no choice,' Fiona had told Betty more than once. 'I know he was very upset about going without speaking to you.'

Believing that Fiona only said it to

make her feel better, Betty had just smiled and thanked her.

* * *

Finally, at the beginning of 1945, just after the New Year, Eddie returned to Midchester. He had been there several days before Betty knew about it, and then it was only from gossip and whispers. On a crisp January morning, Eddie called at the pub just before closing time and asked Betty to go for a walk with him.

She was genuinely pleased to see him. She had hoped, however, that the moment she did see him, she would be overwhelmed by love. It was a fantasy she had entertained for many nights when the thought of Ben became too painful to bear. As it was, she felt nothing but the pleasure in seeing an old friend alive and well.

The years had changed Eddie, as had his injuries. He had lost the gangly look of youth and filled out quite a lot. A large angry scar marred his once-clear forehead, and he had lost some of his hair.

'I'm so glad to see you, Eddie,' Betty said as they walked through Midchester together.

They were a few paces apart, awkward and almost like strangers. It was hard to believe that they had once dashed through the streets together as children then as teenagers.

'It's good to see you too, Betty,' he replied. 'It's been a long time.'

'Yes, it has.'

'Sorry I didn't write, but . . . '

'Don't worry. Your mum explained. It must have been terrifying, not knowing who you were.'

'Yes, it was. Then things started coming back in bits. Fragments of things and people, and what have you.'

'I can imagine. Well, I can't, but you know what I mean.'

'So when Mum mentioned you when she came to see me last year, I didn't know who you were!'

That was not quite what she expected to hear, and she examined her feelings for a moment to see whether she was hurt about Eddie forgetting her. She was not. She found she was merely slightly put out.

'Oh, well, that's understandable.'

Perhaps that's what Mrs Simpson had not wanted to tell her. That Eddie could not even remember who she was. Myrtle had probably thought it would hurt Betty's feelings.

'I bet you remembered your mum, though.'

'Not straight away,' Eddie said. 'I remembered . . . ' He paused. 'Little bits of things.'

'How is your memory now?'

'I remember when we used to go scrumping up at Bedlington Farm. As kids, you know?'

'Don't tell Mr Armstrong that. He won't let me up there any more.' Betty tried to laugh, but it came out forced. 'I've been working up there for the war effort, you know. Not the same as you, in the thick of it, but I like to think we've made a difference.' She realised she was waffling. 'What are you planning to do now you're home?'

They were nearing the Simpson cottage, and she had a strange feeling that he would soon say goodbye to her and go back inside. It worried her, because nothing was really resolved. Was Eddie afraid to speak to her about their promise? She wondered if his mother had expected her to be the one to tell him about it. If so, Betty hardly knew where to start.

'Actually, Betty, as soon as the war is over I'm going back to France.'

'France?'

'Yes. Someone I know has a farm there. I've got some experience, as you know, from working with dad on Bedlington Farm, so I think I can make a go of it.'

'So you're going into business with your friend?'

'Yes. Sort of. Betty, a lot has happened since I left.'

'Yes, I know.'

'But Mum said you'd found someone else, so it shouldn't really matter.'

'What shouldn't matter?'

Before Eddie could reply a woman came out of the Simpson house. She was about twenty-seven years old, and she carried a child of about four.

'Eddie, 'ave you told the mademoiselle?'

'No, not yet, Veronique, I was just getting to it.'

'Told me what?'

Betty looked from the woman to Eddie, then to the child, and realisation began to dawn.

'We are married. And this is our child, Edward.'

The Wait Is Over

'Mum said I should tell you. She reckoned that I owed it to you or something. I'm sorry if it came out a bit harsh, Betty, but I barely remember you at all. Anyway, Mum said you'd got yourself another fella pretty quickly, so no harm done, eh?'

'Quickly?' Betty put her hands on her hips. 'Quickly! I waited four years for you to return, Eddie Simpson, and for two of those I thought you were dead. Yet still I waited because it's what your mum and dad wanted.'

Eddie and his wife looked at her wide-eyed, but she carried on regardless, letting all her anger and frustration come out.

'I let go my only chance of happiness with the man I loved because your mother and father kept reminding me of my promise to you. You, on the other hand, judging by the age of your son, seemed to have forgotten me the moment you landed in France four years ago, never mind when you were injured!'

She started to laugh, hysterically, until tears fell from her eyes.

'I can't believe how stupid I've been!'

'Now, then,' Eddie said. 'Me and Veronique just had a bond, that's all. I wanted to write and tell you, but, well to be honest I didn't know if I'd ever see her again, what with the war and that. Truth is, she were the first person I remembered. She told me she'd wait for me and she did. With our lad.'

Any other time, Betty might have thought that was very romantic, but whilst Eddie had the excuse of amnesia for the second half of his disappearance from her life, he could hardly use that to explain how he managed to meet another woman only weeks after extracting a promise from Betty.

'Well, you certainly kept your options open, Eddie. I'll give you that! How many more girls did you persuade to promise they'd wait for you?'

It was a cheap shot, but Betty was glad to see it struck home.

'Now, then,' Eddie said again. 'There's no need to be like that.'

'No, you're right, there isn't,' Betty said, shame-faced. 'I wish you and your wife and that beautiful child every happiness, really I do. So long, Eddie. Veronique.'

Betty turned and walked away. As she did, she heard Veronique's waspish voice.

'You told me this Betty girl was not that pretty!'

'Well, I forgot what she looked like, didn't I, *ma cherie*?' In Eddie's flat vowels it came out 'ma cherry', much to Betty's amusement.

'You are telling me that a man forgets a girl like that?' This was followed by a volley of French that Betty suspected would not be very polite in English.

She laughed all the way home.

★ ★ ★

The war ended. First there was Victory in Europe, and then Victory in Japan. The men and boys who survived the war started to come home to their towns and villages, and the nation laughed and cried in equal measure. Though the Allies had won the war, there was little sign of it in the hardships that followed.

Only when the war ended properly did Tom and Maggie set a proper date for their wedding, in the spring of 1946.

'Are you all packed then, love?' Tom asked, standing at Betty's bedroom door on the morning of the wedding.

'Yes, just a few more things, and then I'll be out of your hair.'

She continued cramming things into her suitcase, hoping she wouldn't need another one. It was a long trip to London with several changes, and she didn't want to be dragging lots of luggage around.

'You don't have to go, you know.

Maggie doesn't want to push you out!'

'I know, Dad. But you'll not want me hanging around when you're newly-weds!'

'I wish you didn't have to go so far away, Betty. Surely you could find yourself some digs and a job in Shrewsbury. I don't like to think of you off in the big city alone.'

'I want to go to London, Dad. It's time to start a new life for myself. Anyway, I told you, Daisy and Rosie's mum and dad have said I can rent a room from them, so I won't be alone. And I won't be short of work. The professor has put in a good word for me at one of the museums, and if all else fails, there are plenty of pubs in London. I know how to pull a pint better than anyone. I've had a good teacher!'

'I know you think we let you down, love.'

'Don't, Dad.' Betty put her hand up. 'That was a long time ago, and it's all over now.'

'I'm not sure it is. I feel as though I've lost my girl because of it.'

Tears stung her eyes. Things had changed between them, but he was still her dad and she still loved him.

'That'll never happen, Dad. No matter what.' She sat on the edge of the bed. 'I need to get away. I spent all that time waiting, and now I don't have to wait for anyone any more.'

If, in her heart, she still waited for Ben, she kept it to herself. Nothing good would come of that, hence the move to London.

Tom came and sat next to her.

'There's always a home for you here, sweetheart. You know that, don't you? Me marrying Maggie today isn't going to change that. She thinks the world of you, and she's afraid you're leaving because you think she's going to turn into a wicked stepmother.'

'I don't think that at all. I think the world of Maggie, too. She makes you happy, and it makes me feel better to know you won't be alone when I'm in London.'

'You'll come back and see your old dad from time to time, won't you?'

'Of course I will.'

And yet, as she said it, Betty realised she might be lying. The way she felt at that moment, she never wanted to see Midchester again. It held too many memories for her; some good, some bad. Even the good memories, of Ben and the short time they had, were too painful. She was reminded of those in every brick of every house and every tree that had started to blossom.

Sometimes she wished she had Eddie's amnesia, even though in the short time he returned, before he went to France with his wife, it was clear that it could be very selective. In fact, she became convinced she was the only one in Midchester he had forgotten, judging by the way he greeted everyone else like an old friend, but struggled to remember even the most innocent things about Betty. Especially when his wife was around!

Betty had to concede it was a handy excuse for ignoring awkward subjects one did not want to think about. If only she could wipe Ben from her memory as easily. But she had come to realise that he was quite unforgettable.

'I think I might go out for a walk to say goodbye to the old place,' she told her father. 'Don't worry, I'll be back in time for the wedding.'

Wearing her best blue suit, Betty stepped out into watery sunlight. It was not very warm yet, but the signs of spring were unmistakable. Daffodils had started to emerge from their winter sleep, and the trees were starting to blossom.

For a moment, Betty felt a pang of regret about leaving Midchester. It really was the prettiest village in England. But it had also become something of a waiting-room for Betty, and she was eager to see what lay beyond, now that the war was over and she had a chance to live again.

She wandered along the main street, past the square. Myrtle Simpson was standing at Mrs Baker's garden gate, nattering. Herbie's wooing of Mrs Baker had given her some status in the village, and they were due to be married in a few months' time.

'And now they've had a little girl,' Myrtle was telling Mrs Baker. 'Natalie. Though it sounds so much better in a French accent. Eddie practically runs his father-in-law's farm. They were in the Resistance, you know, Veronique and her family! That's how Eddie met them. Veronique saved his life.' Seeing Betty approaching, Myrtle lowered her voice, but not quite low enough. 'Of course, I do think that some might have been a little more understanding of the situation. Especially when they're in no position to throw stones.'

Like many people who had been in the wrong and for a very long time, Myrtle Simpson had turned the tables and decided that Betty was the one at fault. She had been heard to say that Eddie only fell in love with Veronique because he had guessed Betty would not really wait for him, forgetting that waiting was exactly what Betty had done until Ben arrived in the village.

Betty smiled to herself, because soon nothing Mrs Simpson said would matter anymore. She would be gone from the village.

'Good morning, Mrs Simpson. Mrs Baker.'

To her credit, Mrs Baker looked embarrassed by Mrs Simpson's words. Betty guessed that as Mrs Baker had often been harshly judged for her own chaotic lifestyle bringing up children alone, she was less inclined to think bad things about Betty. It perhaps explained why she had taken Herbie Potter into her heart.

'Good morning, Betty, pet,' she said. 'You're looking very smart and pretty today. Are you looking forward to the wedding?'

'Yes, very much so,' Betty replied,

walking past them. 'I hope to see you there.'

'We'll be there.'

Despite Betty's misgivings about Herbie Potter attending her father's wedding, she could hardly say anything, since he was Maggie's brother and he was giving her away. So Betty had bitten her tongue, all the time reminding herself that soon she would be gone from Midchester, and she did not want to leave under a cloud.

'I hear Michael is going to sing in the choir,' Betty commented.

'Yes, he is. Poor little thing hardly says a word, but you get him singing ... It was your friends, Daisy and Rosie, who found that out. How are they, by the way?'

'They're very well. Glad to be back home with their mum, I think, but they're talking about going to Europe and helping to get things back on their feet. I hardly recognise them from the two giggly girls who came to the farm.'

'The war has made us all grow up,'

Mrs Baker said.

Mrs Simpson coughed, clearly not too happy to have been ignored.

'Well let's hope that one twin — what's her name? Daisy? Let's hope she can behave herself with the men over there.'

On the basis that Betty did not want to leave the village under a cloud, she ignored the insult to her sweet young friend and simply smiled a good morning and walked on.

She was near Peg's cottage when she saw Herbie coming out of Peg's, having delivered the post.

'Morning, Betty.'

'Morning, Mr Potter.'

'I think it can be Herbie, now we're to be related, don't you?'

'Hmm,' Betty said.

Herbie closed Peg's garden gate and took his hat off, running his hands through his hair.

'I know you've not much reason to like me, Betty. I don't blame you for that. It's stupid what love makes a person do. But I'm really sorry for what I did.' He ran his hands through his hair again. 'Look, can we have a chat? We can sit on that old bench over there.'

'Very well.' For her father and Maggie's sake, she felt she ought to try and get on with Herbie. If only for today.

Herbie looked across to Mrs Baker who gave him a smile and a nod of encouragement.

'She's a good woman, you know,' Herbie said when they sat down. Touchingly he had brushed Betty's part of the seat with his hat. 'Martha, I mean.'

'Yes, I know.'

'She tries so hard and doesn't always get it right, but still, she keeps on trying. And all on her own, too, until we started seeing each other. She's still independent, mind you.'

'Is that what you wanted to discuss with me, Mr Potter.'

'Herbie.'

'Herbie.'

'No, I wanted to explain about what I did. Not that I'm making excuses, mind you. I did wrong. I know that. It's just that Floss went off with that American.'

'I know that. Her and thousands of other women, if we believe the newspapers.'

'Well, I asked her to come back, you see. Even with the little babby, I told her we could pretend it was mine and I'd bring him up as my own.'

'That was nice of you.' Betty realised that this was a side to Herbie that she had never seen.

'It wouldn't have made a bit of difference to me, because I loved her, you see. And I'd never have treated the little one anything other than as my own. But she had this thing that Harry was going to come for her when he knew about the boy. He didn't, of course.

'Well, it was after I got that letter, telling me that she wouldn't marry me even for the sake of her baby, that it happened. It was a daft thing, really, that first time. I just happened to see a pair of stockings on the line and snatched at them, because they reminded me of her and him. Then I started doing it more often and it became a bit of a compulsion. You know the rest, Betty. On the night Harry run off with that young girl, I thought I'd done right in lending you the van to help her, but when I had to deliver post up at the airbase early the next morning, I got a bit angry about it all again. Why should he just keep hurting our women like that? I know I'm not the sort of man that women see as romantic, but I've got a lot of love for the right one.'

'And now you've found her.'

Betty felt choked. Peg was right. Things weren't always just black and white. It didn't excuse what Herbie did, but it did explain why he could act so rashly in a moment of madness. And it was good of him to want to take on a child that wasn't his, to save

Floss from shame.

'Let's forget about it, Mr Potter . . . Herbie.' Betty smiled. 'I don't want anything to spoil Dad's day today.'

'No, me neither. I know me and Tom have had our differences, but he's a good man and I know he'll take care of our Maggie. She thinks the world of him, you know. And you. She cares a lot about you, lass.'

'I love her dearly, too.'

'She'll be glad to know that. So let's shake hands and be friends for Tom and Maggie's sake, eh?'

Betty held out her hand.

'Very well. We'll be friends . . . Herbie.'

In forgiving him, Betty felt herself set free from all the dark thoughts that had haunted her since Herbie was found out and apparently forgiven by the villagers. A huge sigh of relief swept from her, clearing some of the dark clouds from above her head.

'Actually, we'll be relatives. I'll be your stepuncle! And very proud to be.

You're a good girl, Betty. You always have been, never mind what the Simpsons say. I'm sorry you lost your fella.'

'I don't care that Eddie got married, Herbie.'

'I meant the other one. Captain Greenwood.'

'Oh!' That choked Betty up even more. 'Well, obviously that wasn't meant to be.'

'Don't be so sure of that, pet. Well, I'd better get on if I'm to make our Maggie's wedding.'

★　★　★

Herbie went on down the road, whistling. Betty suspected that he too felt happier now they had cleared the air. Perhaps now that she was leaving Midchester it was a good time to forgive and forget the past. Otherwise the dark clouds might follow her wherever she went.

Before Betty could go much further, Peg came from her house.

'That was a nice thing you did there, dear,' she said. 'Herbie has been worried about you.'

'Why should he have cared what I think?'

'Because you're the sort of person that people want to like them.'

'Am I, Peg? I've never been aware of that.'

'Oh, come on, why do you think the twins took to you so easily? I don't think anyone else could have turned them around the way you did. How is the terrible twosome, by the way?'

'Not so terrible nowadays. They've grown up a lot, I think. They're back in London, looking for work. I know the men who returned from the war needed jobs, but it was a bit much that all the women who'd kept the fields ploughed were thrown out of theirs as soon as the war ended!'

'That's the way of war, dear.'

'I'd better get on with this walk,' Betty said. 'Otherwise I'll miss Dad's wedding.'

'Are we all right, Betty?'

'What do you mean?'

For the first time in ages, Betty looked at Peg's face. She seemed to have aged over the past few years. She was frailer than she had been.

'I mean, do you forgive your old friend, Peg, too?'

'There's nothing to forgive, Peg. We'll always be friends, I hope.'

Peg nodded.

'That's my hope too. Promise me — no, I shouldn't say that. Your life has been ruined enough by promises.'

'Go on, Peg, what did you want to say?'

'Promise me that when you're far away you won't forget us here.'

'I'm hardly like to forget my dad. And, anyway, I'm only going to London. It's not like I won't be able to come back sometimes.'

'Hmm,' Peg said mysteriously.

Once again Betty had that feeling of others knowing something she did not.

'I won't forget you, Peg. How could

I? You are Midchester to me and to many others around here.'

'Thank you.' Peg's eyes became watery. 'Goodness.' She laughed. 'I think my hay fever is coming on early. Go on, be off on your walk before I make a fool of myself.'

Betty reached over the gate and kissed Peg on the cheek.

'We are friends, Peg, and always will be.'

Another cloud seemed to shift from above Betty's head. Her friendship with Peg had meant everything to her, yet she had neglected it for a while because of her anger about Herbie being let off with his crime. She wondered what it would take for all the clouds to go.

She walked through the churchyard, stopping at her mother's grave to ask her to bless Tom and Maggie's marriage. She knew her mother would do so, but it felt good to talk to her for what might be the last time. And then she took the back gate along the path towards Bedlington Hall.

As she walked the path, she was reminded of Housman's poem and what she had said to Ben about it not being the same path twice. That much was true. It looked the same, and led in the same direction, but for her it had changed. She was different to the girl who had walked it with Ben two years earlier. She was no longer waiting, and that was good.

But there was also emptiness in her heart. That was the last cloud, which she felt it would take a miracle to lift.

She was walking with her head down when someone spoke in a soft, Scottish lilt.

'Don't bother saying hello, then!'

Betty looked up to see Fiona and Charlie, walking hand in hand towards her. They looked very happy and very much in love.

'Hello! I was lost in thought — what are you two doing here?'

'We're coming to your dad's wedding,' Charlie replied. 'It's official. We got an invitation.'

'That's wonderful! Come on, we'll go back together,' Betty said.

'Er, why don't you carry on with your walk, and we'll see you there?' Fiona said.

'Yes, my wife and I want a little alone time,' Charlie announced.

'Wife?'

Fiona held out her hand to show her wedding ring.

'We married in London yesterday, by special licence. I'm going back with Charlie to Wisconsin. Wherever on Earth that is!' Fiona laughed, looking prettier than ever.

Betty hugged them both, and began to feel tears were nearer than ever.

'I'm so happy for you,' she said, wiping her eyes. 'So I will leave you alone for a while. But don't disappear after the wedding. I want to know all the news.'

Unspoken was the knowledge that she wanted to know about Ben. She almost asked Charlie then, but shyness prevented her.

We're not rushing off yet,' Charlie gave Betty another hug.

'Are you all right, Charlie?' she asked, remembering his psychological problems.

'I'm getting there, Betty. With Fiona's help.' He squeezed his young wife's hand. 'I told her that's why she has to come to Wisconsin with me. No other nurse will do for me.'

'I should think not!'

Betty laughed. What a strange day it was turning out to be.

'Then I'll leave you both alone.'

She waved and carried on walking up towards Bedlington Hall. She was halfway along the route when she saw a tall figure walking towards her. The world seemed to freeze, and his steps seemed too slow.

Betty stood stock still, not daring to move in case he should turn out to be a mirage.

'Ben!' she said, breathlessly. He looked as handsome as ever, albeit a little thinner and paler.

'Hi, Betty.'

'What — how? Are you coming to Dad's wedding too?'

'I got my invitation, all proper and above board, as you Brits say.'

'No-one said. I mean, Dad didn't tell me. It's nice to see you.'

She mentally kicked herself for such a lame response. What she really wanted to do was run into his arms and kiss him, but she did not know if he would welcome such contact.

'Are you well?'

'I'm very well. How are you?'

'Oh, I'm well, too. So you finally made it to Berlin, then?'

'Yeah, and beyond. But I don't want to talk about that on a day like today.'

Betty nodded her understanding. She had heard many tales of the horrors that awaited the Allies when they liberated Germany and beyond.

'Eddie got married,' she blurted out.

'You're not heartbroken?'

'What? Oh, no. I was a little annoyed at first because . . . Never mind. How you know, anyway?'

'I got letters. From your dad, Maggie and Peg. Then Mr Simpson wrote. That was strange. Even Herbie the postman sent me a letter.'

'They did?'

'Yeah. The only person who didn't write and tell me was you. I waited. I hoped you'd write, Betty.'

'I'm sorry. I wanted to, but the way you left . . . I thought you didn't care about ever seeing me again, and that it would make no difference if Eddie were married or not.'

'Tell me why you were annoyed with Eddie. Are you sure it wasn't because you loved him?'

'No! That wasn't it.' Betty's tears began to fall. 'I was . . . I'd given up so much waiting for him. I'd given you up, and I didn't know how to get you back and . . . '

Betty didn't have to say anymore, because Ben had taken her in his arms and was kissing her.

'I've been such a fool,' he said when

he'd finished. 'I left the way I did because I didn't want to tear you apart in the way the Simpsons had. I wanted you to be free to make the choice to stay with him if you wanted to. I've regretted it ever since. I regretted not telling you to forget Eddie. But mostly I regret not telling you how much I love you.'

'You do? Really? Oh, Ben, I love you, too.'

'I loved you from the moment I walked into the pub and asked for a pint of your finest ale. I especially loved the look on your face. You really wanted to laugh, but you were so polite.' Ben laughed. 'Do you remember that?'

'Yes. I loved you then, too, only I was too stupid to admit it to myself.'

'I know it's a lot to ask, and all this is very sudden, but will you come to America with me? We can get married as soon as you want. Maybe with a special licence like Fiona and Charlie. How do you feel about being a New York City cop's wife?'

can't think of anything I'd like
more!'

They walked hand-in-hand back towards the church, just as the celebrants were arriving for the wedding. For the first time, Betty felt she could walk in the sunlight with Ben instead of hiding away her love for him.

The very last cloud lifted from above her head. She hugged her father, Maggie and Peg, whispering thanks to them. They had protected her all along, and she had failed to appreciate it. She even hugged Herbie, and immediately saw that a few clouds lifted from over his head, too.

As her father and Maggie said their vows, Betty and Ben sat in a pew, hand in hand, stealing happy glances at each other, and silently practising the vows they were going to be making very soon.

Their day had come at last.

THE END

We do hope that you have enjoyed reading this large print book.

Did you know that all of our titles are available for purchase?

We publish a wide range of high quality large print books including:
Romances, Mysteries, Classics
General Fiction
Non Fiction and Westerns

Special interest titles available in large print are:
The Little Oxford Dictionary
Music Book, Song Book
Hymn Book, Service Book

Also available from us courtesy of Oxford University Press:
Young Readers' Dictionary
(large print edition)
Young Readers' Thesaurus
(large print edition)

For further information or a free brochure, please contact us at:
Ulverscroft Large Print Books Ltd.,
The Green, Bradgate Road, Anstey,
Leicester, LE7 7FU, England.
Tel: (00 44) 0116 236 4325
Fax: (00 44) 0116 234 0205

THE FAMILY AT FARRSHORE

Kate Blackadder

After breaking up with Daniel, archaeologist Cathryn Fenton quite happily travels to Farrshore in Scotland to work on a major dig. In the driving rain, she gives a lift to Canadian Magnus Macaskill, then finds that they both lodge at the same place. The dig goes well, with Magnus filming the proceedings for a Viking series. But trouble looms in Farrshore — starting when Magnus learns that his son Tyler is coming over from Canada to be with his dad . . .

THE TEMP AND THE TYCOON

Liz Fielding

Talie Calhoun had briefly met billionaire Jude Radcliffe whilst working as a temp at the Radcliffe Group. It was a rare holiday away from nursing her invalid mother. But when she's asked to accompany Mr Radcliffe to New York, she is over the moon. However, Radcliffe is furious with his secretary's choice of temp. But Talie is a vibrant woman and, as he becomes drawn to her, Jude becomes determined to take care of her and make her his own.

LOVE TRIUMPHANT

Margaret Mounsdon

Steve Baxter disappears while interior designer Lizzie Hilton is working on the refurbishment of his property. His brother, Todd, suspects Lizzie of becoming romantically involved with Steve, knowing that he is due to come into an inheritance upon marriage. Lizzie challenges Todd to find evidence to substantiate his outrageous allegation. But when Paul Owen appears on the scene Lizzie panics — because Paul can provide Todd with the evidence he is looking for . . .

FORGET-ME-NOT

Jasmina Svenne

As girls, Diana Aspley and Alice Simmonds swore that they would be friends forever. So Diana is devastated when she receives the news that Alice has died in unexplained circumstances. Then during her first London Season, she thinks she catches sight of a familiar figure from a carriage window . . . Diana is determined to get to the truth about Alice's fate, even if she has to persuade the aloof and eminently eligible Edgar Godolphin to help her.

RETURN TO BARRADALE

Carol MacLean

Melody has sworn never to return to Barradale, the island where she'd grown up — and been so unhappy . . . Now, living in Glasgow, she has forged a new life in the City for herself. But when the gorgeous Kieran Matthews turns up on her doorstep, demanding that she should go back with him to see her sick sister, she finds she cannot refuse. And for Melody, family secrets must be unravelled before Kieran's love can help to resolve her past.